PRISON OF NIGHT

The woman standing against the parapet couldn't be for real for Dumarest had seen her lying dead on a world far distant in time and space and yet, as he watched, she smiled at him and extended her hands. Lallia stepped towards him. Against the sky her hair was a mass of shining ebon. "Earl?" And then she was gone and, again, he was alone.

Delusia – the time when the dead walked and talked and communed with the living. A planetary insanity of which he was a part . . . if it was an insanity.

"Earl!" Another figure standing where the other had been but this time one with hair of a sombre red. Kalin? As he rose he recognised the woman. Not Kalin but Dephine. Another who had played him false.

"Do you still hate me, Earl? I intended to sell you to the Cyclan . . . And still you do not hate? She blurred as he made no answer . . .

Also in Arrow by E. C. Tubb

THE DUMAREST SAGA

E. C. TUBB

Prison of Night

ARROW BOOKS

Arrow Books Ltd
3 Fitzroy Square, London W1P 6JD

An imprint of the Hutchinson Publishing Group

London Melbourne Sydney Auckland
Wellington Johannesburg and agencies
throughout the world

First published 1977
Arrow edition 1980

© E. C. Tubb 1977

Made and printed in Great Britain
by The Anchor Press Ltd
Tiptree, Essex

ISBN 0 09 923970 1

Chapter ONE

Kars Gartok was the last to leave, lingering in his cabin until the others had gone, unwilling to engage in useless conversation, to hear again the empty threats and bitter denunciations. Only when the ship was silent did he venture forth to step through the open port and head down the ramp to the field below. It was late in the day, the sun low on the horizon, the air misted with a damp fog which pearled the mesh of the perimeter fence and gave the tall figure standing just beyond the gate a blurred, ethereal quality as if it were the figment of a dream.

But Brother Eldon was no ghost. He waited, dressed in a brown, homespun robe the cowl thrown back despite the chill to reveal a face seamed and creased with age and privation. His feet were bare in open sandals and gnarled hands gripped a bowl of cheap plastic chipped and scarred by usage and time. He lifted it as Gartok approached.

"Of your charity, brother."

Halting Gartok stared at the monk then said, dryly, "Charity? Aren't there fools enough on Ilyard without you wanting more?"

"Is to give an act of foolishness?"

"What else?"

"Some would call it an act of virtue, brother."

"To give without hope of reward is the act of a fool," said Gartok, curtly. "A lesson a man in my trade quickly learns."

"As those did who left the ship before you?" Then, before Gartok could answer, the monk added, quietly, "It could be that you have already had your reward. You seem uninjured and you are alive."

"Yes," said Gartok, heavily. "I'm alive."

He was a big man, wide of shoulder and thick of neck,

5

dressed in dark leather trimmed with scarlet, polished patches showing at shoulders and waist where body-armor had rested. His temples bore callouses from the weight of a helmet and his eyes, deep-set and hooded, watched from beneath beetling brows. His hands were broad, the fingers spatulate, the knuckles knobs of bone. His face matched the hands, broad, rough, ridged and seamed with scars. The mouth was a trap, the chin a rock, the nose a predatory beak. He looked what he was—a professional dealer in death.

Watching him as he stood there, the mist dewing the stubble of his cropped head, the monk said, "What happened, brother?"

"We lost."

"And?"

"What more needs to be said? We were out-gunned, out-manned, out-maneuvered. Eighty-three of a hundred died on Craig. The details? What do they matter?"

"Even so, brother, I would like to know."

For a moment the mercenary hesitated then, shrugging, said, "It's the old story; two men snarling at each other over a strip of land on a world not worth a woman's spit. Each turned to force and hired men. A minor war and dangerous only to those involved. Or so it should have been but accidents happen. And the locals were stubborn and refused to evacuate their villages."

And so they had died in blossoms of flame as shells had burst in crude houses and fragmentation bombs had torn air and flesh with whining shards of metal. An old story and one common on Ilyard where men came to talk and rest and seek employment. Common too on worlds cursed with ambitious rulers who thought of men as pawns to be used in a complicated game.

"Craig," said the monk. "You said that was the name of the world?"

"Yes. One lying on the edge of the Rift. A bleak place of rock and water and cold. A world where the rich burn turf to keep warm and the poor huddle together. But one the wealthier now for the bodies of good men fertilizing the soil."

"But you are not one of them, brother," reminded the

monk and lifted his empty bowl a little. "Those who give to the poor often enjoy good fortune."

A direct appeal to the superstition inherent in all gamblers, and what was a mercenary but a man who gambled with his life? Yet the monk felt no pride of achievement as Gartok plunged a hand into a pocket. Trained in the art of psychology it was simple for him to manipulate the emotional triggers which all men carried and to which they could not help but to respond. And the mercenary, like all his breed, must have inner weaknesses, hidden guilts, invisible cracks in his external armor of competence.

As he threw coins into the bowl Gartok said, "It's all I can give, monk. If it isn't enough to buy a blessing at least spare me your curse."

"I curse no one, brother."

"Then you are more saint than man. I curse people often. Captain Blasco who has a taste for killing. The fool who hired us. The swine who—well, never mind. What is done is done and what point to dwell in the past? But you, Brother, have you any news?" Then, as the monk made no reply, "I forgot, you do not trade in war. But at least tell me this—have any persons of consequence and wealth arrived recently? High lords with ambition and money to hire men?" His eyes narrowed as they searched the old face. Like the monk he had a knowledge of psychology but could read nothing. Then a flicker of the eyes gave him a clue. "They have? You do not deny it? Good. Fortune could be smiling on me at last. Where are they staying?"

"You can find out where, brother," said the monk. "As you say, I do not trade in war."

He shivered a little as the mercenary strode away, the wind was increasing and its chill numbed skin and bone. He could barely feel the bowl in his hands and his feet were like blocks of wood yet he welcomed the discomfort as a reminder of times past when, as a young man newly taken into the Church, he had stood before gates like this begging for alms.

An essential duty but one which he no longer had need to perform but old habits died hard and, always, it was necessary to guard against the sin of pride.

And to beg was to be humble.

A gust of wind caught his robe and drove it hard against his body, the damp material emphasizing the chill of the dying day. From the distance came the shouts of men and the monotonous pounding of feet. Raw recruits were at drill; men engaged on a scatter of worlds and transported here to Ilyard where their contracts were sold at a profit. Those who had already been bloodied, who had been flung into combat and who had managed to survive, fetched a higher price than the rest. Others, like Kars Gartok, long freed of contractual restraint, sold their skills to any who would be willing to pay. Their skill and loyalty for what it was worth, going out to fight, to kill, to bleed, to die if they must to live if they could even at the cost of all they owned.

One day, thought the monk, he might be able to understand what drove men to act in such a manner, but for now it was cold, the field was empty and work still waited to be done.

The shadows were lengthening as he reached the first of a litter of shacks and huts which sprawled away from the town to the side of the field. Lowtowns were all the same no matter on which world they were found. The refuge of the desperate, those stricken with illness, those cursed with poverty. The stench of it rose like a miasma from the ramshackle dwellings; constructions of scrap and discarded plastic, of fabrics salvaged from the garbage of the more fortunate, doing little but to keep out the rain and giving a scrap of privacy.

The church was little better, but from intent rather than need. A building of brick or stone with solid walls and barred windows, of thick doors and heated air would have been an affront to those it had been designed to serve. As a monk wearing silk and gems would have insulted the wretch to whom he preached the virtue of poverty. To gain the confidence of those in need they had to be met at their own level.

Yet, even so, the church was bigger and better than others he had known. They had been the flimsy shacks of portable churches: fabric and poles which could be carried on a back together with the benediction light which was the heart of the structure. Yet tent or palace all were the same. All strove to teach the same message. To persuade all who came to listen or who could be persuaded to pay attention to accept the Universal teaching of complete Brotherhood. That no man was an island. That the pain of one was the pain of all. That all shared the burden of a common heritage. That all belonged to the *Corpus Humanite*. That once each could look at the other and say, *there, but for the grace of God, go I*, the millennium would have arrived.

He would never see it. No monk now alive would ever see it. Men bred too fast and travelled too far for that. They rested on too many worlds scattered throughout the galaxy and were subjected to too many strains. But, eventually, it would come. It was an article of faith to believe that. The purpose of his being.

"Brother!" A man rose from where he'd been squatting in the dirt and mud at the side of the track. He was thin, his face yellowed with jaundice, his teeth chattering with cold. He smelt of suppurating pus; the sickly sweet odor of tissue-decay. The hand he extended was like a claw, thin, quivering. "Brother. For the love of God help me!"

"Ask, brother, and if it is possible it will be given."

"I'm ill. Rotten with sores and something else. Starving. I can't get work. And I—I've . . ."

"The church is waiting," said Brother Eldon quietly. "Enter it, kneel beneath the benediction light, confess and receive forgiveness. Medicines are available and they will be given."

"Brother, will you speak for me to Major Khaftle? He—"

"One thing at a time, brother." Eldon was insistent. "First you must be given what help we have. After, well, we shall see. Come now."

He took the quivering claw into his hand, feeling the febrile heat of the skin, recognizing the fever, the disease. The man was dying and would die despite the antibiotics they could give. But he would not die alone and he would die in peace. Brother Veac would see to that.

The young monk accepted his charge and glanced sharply at his superior. It was not his place to question or to criticize, but he would not have been human had he not made a comment.

"It is late, brother, and cold."

"Yes."

"There is food and warmth within. You should rest now."

"And stop trying to act the young man, brother?" Eldon smiled as the other looked abashed. "Am I so old you think I have forgotten to remember how I thought when young? Take care of our friend now. Is Brother Biul available? Good." Then lowering his voice he whispered, "The infirmary, I think. There is room? Then see he has a place. I fear that he will not be with us for long."

But first came the easing of his heart and soul. To kneel beneath the swirling bowl of colored light, to drift into a hypnotic condition, to unburden himself, to suffer subjective penance and then to be given the bread of forgiveness. And if most of those coming to the church did so for the sake of the wafer of concentrates then it was a fair exchange. For each who knelt beneath the light was conditioned not to kill.

"Brother!" Biul looked up from where he sat busy with papers and rose as Eldon entered the office. "You must be frozen! Why must you be so stubborn? You are too old to act this way."

Older than Veac the monk cared less for diplomacy and long friendship had given him a casual familiarity. Now he bustled around, fetching a warm blanket, filling a bowl with soup, standing over Eldon while he ate. Only when the bowl was empty did he permit the older man to speak.

"Biul, you have all the attributes of a bully," said Eldon mildly. "If I didn't know you meant well I might even be annoyed."

"As I will be unless you take better care of yourself. We need you—and do I have to remind you that self-injury is a sin?" Biul cleared away the bowl, rearranged the blanket then said, "Well?"

"Little. A few coins."

"And?"

"Bad news." Eldon felt his shoulders sag. "War on Craig. The first engagements are over but there will be others that is certain. Help will be needed. Contact the seminary on Pace and have them notify those on Hope. A full medical team if possible, as many monks as they can

spare at least. And perhaps influence could be brought to
bear on those responsible to cease the hostilities."

It was possible, the Church had friends in high places,
and it would be tried, but inevitably there would be delays
and in a war-situation delay meant suffering, disease, degradation and death.

To alleviate a little of it was the most they could hope
to do.

As Biul left Eldon sank back in his chair, conscious of
the warmth of the blanket, the snug comfort of the room.
It was bleak enough, the walls ornamented with small me-
mentoes and a few paintings of worlds known when
young, but it held everything he had come to value since,
when a youth, he had applied for acceptance into the
church and had commenced his training.

There was trust there, and faith, and the desire of one
to help another. There was truth and tolerance and com-
passion. There was an acknowledgement that life was
more than could be seen on the surface and that, without
the belief in something greater than Man, then Man could
not be greater than what he was.

A point on which he had argued when young and had
still not understood what it really meant to be a monk.

Brother Hoji had stripped away his illusions.

He was old, stooped, withered, crippled, acid. He was in
charge of indoctrination and had not been gentle. Leaning
back, half-asleep, Eldon could hear again the voice which
had rasped like a file through the confines of the room
into which had been packed a score of youngsters like
himself.

"Why did you apply to become monks? What motive
drives you? That question must be answered before any
other. Look into the mirror of your soul and search for
the truth. Is it in order to help your fellow man? Is it that
and nothing more? If not then you don't belong here. You
are wasting my time and your own. Rise and leave and
none will think the worst of you. Be honest. Above all, be
honest!"

Someone had coughed; strain triggering a near-hysteri-
cal giggle covered too late into the resemblance of a normal expulsion of air.

"You!" The twisted fingers of the old monk had been an

accusing claw. "You laughed—why? Did you think I was
a fool? That I tended to exaggerate? That I distorted the
truth? Don't bother to answer." Then, in a lower voice, he
had continued. "If you hope for personal reward or high
office or the love and respect of those you are dedicated to
serve, then you do not belong here. If you yearn for power
or pain the same applies. Pain you will get and discomfort
and suffering. You will know disappointment and see the
work of years destroyed in a moment. You will be scorned
and held in contempt, robbed and beaten, used and ignored, hated and despised. Yet, if in the deepest recesses
of your heart, you long to be so treated, then you have no
place here. Man is not born to suffer. There is no intrinsic
virtue in pain. Those who seek it are enemies of the
Church. If any sit here I tell you now to go. Go!"

No one coughed when he paused, no one giggled, but
still there remained a little doubt. It vanished as the old
monk stripped off his robe and displayed his naked body.
His flesh—and the things which had been done to it.

"God!" whispered the man next to Eldon. "Dear God!"

"The reward of patience," said Hoji. "It happened on
Flackalove. A small settlement that, I thought, had accepted me. For three years I was with them and then
came a drought. Plague followed and children died. They
needed someone to blame." Pausing he donned his robe
then added, quietly, "God gave me the strength to live and
to continue helping my fellows. Now it is safe for a monk
to stay on that world."

Eldon felt again the cold shiver which had touched him
at the calm understatement. How the man must have suffered! The injuries, even though now healed—he could not
bear even now to think of them. Nor understand how the
man had found the courage to continue on the path he
had chosen.

Half the class had left at the end of the first three
months. Half the remainder at the end of the first year. By
the time the training period was over only two others had
stayed together with himself. Three from twenty—a good
average.

And now it was pleasant to sit in the warm and drift
into worlds of memory in which old friends came to greet
him and old places became new again. Even remembered

pain became less demanding, became a part of the joy in serving, of his dedication. And it had not always been pain, though rarely had there been comfort. And now, old, in charge of this church, he could afford to relax a little. To let others share the burden. Others who . . .

After a while Brother Biul came in to rewrap the blanket and to ease the old man's limbs so as to avoid the danger of cramp. He looked, he thought, surprisingly young, the seamed and wrinkled face now plumped a little, the lips curved as if, in his dreams, he smiled.

Then he saw the stillness of the throat, the flaccidity of the great arteries and knew the old man would never smile again.

"Dead?" Kars Gartok frowned. "The old monk dead? But how? I was talking to him only hours ago."

"I know." The officer was polite. "That is why I am here. A routine matter, you understand. A formality. Did he say anything? Complain of feeling unwell, perhaps?"

"No."

"He mentioned no one who had threatened him?"

"No."

"Your cooperation would be appreciated."

"You're getting it," snapped Gartok. He turned and strode across the room, faced the wall, turned and took three steps back again. Like the hotel the chamber was not of the best, the furnishings worn, the carpet faded, the walls stained. One pane of the window was cracked and the radiator which should have warmed the place was failing in its duty. Even the light was dim. "He was at the gate, begging, you know how the monks operate. We talked for a while, he was eager for news and I gave him what I had. Then I left. Is there suspicion of foul play?"

"No." The officer relaxed and tucked away his notebook. "As I said this is a routine matter. The Church has friends on Ilyard and, well, you understand."

Friends of influence, who else could have given the monks permission to establish themselves here? No planet dedicated to war would welcome those who preached the doctrine of peace. The officer was naturally being cautious.

Gartok said, "How did he die?"

"He was old. He should have known better than to stand in the cold. It could have been the final straw. Personally I think that he'd just lived out his life." The officer glanced around the chamber. "No luck on your last engagement?"

"No."

"Too bad, but we can't all win." He spoke with the casual indifference of a man who couldn't care less. "Well, thank you for your patience. If you're looking for work you could do worse than try the High Endeavour. It's on Secunda Avenue close to Breine."

"I know where it is, but isn't Delthraph in business now?"

"He was shot in an argument last month. Creditors sold his business and the new owner isn't established yet. Try the High Endeavour. It's your best choice."

Like the hotel the place was dingy, a little decayed, a building which had known better times. Luck could have brought them. Money could buy paint and workers to refurbish the exterior. New furnishings would brighten up inside. Rich employers would come to sound out what was offered and winners would make the place their headquarters. Fame followed success and success bred riches. But that had yet to come.

Kars Gartok stepped from the street into the vestibule. A girl smiled at him and a man looked up from where he sat behind a counter. A guard-receptionist, the hand he kept hidden would be holding a weapon. His eyes checked the mercenary, noting the thin cloak, the hat with the feather, the pistol belted at his waist. All were of local manufacture bought less than a couple of hours ago.

"Your first time here?"

Gartok nodded. "I've been away. Delthraph would have known me."

"He's dead."

"That's why I'm here. Upstairs?"

"The front room. You won't be alone. The girl will provide anything you want. Food? Wine?"

"Wine. A flagon."

He mounted the stairs as the girl bustled to fill the order. The room was easy to find and, as the man downstairs had promised, he wouldn't be alone. A dozen men lounged in chairs around a table, light from the fire augmenting the dim glow from lanterns and throwing a dancing ruby light over hard faces, glinting metal, belts, polished leather, the winking gleam of gems.

Halting within the chamber Gartok introduced himself adding, "Have I fought with any here? Against them? No?"

"Once I think," said a man at the far end of the table. "Were you on Lisyen about five years ago? With Donlenck's Destroyers?"

"And if I was?"

"I served with Voronech."

"And lost as I remember." Gartok looked at the man. "Any grudges?"

"Hell, no. I doubt if we ever even met. It was all long-range stuff, right?"

Gartok nodded and, as the girl arrived with his order, slammed the flagon on the table.

"Right. Now have a drink and fill me in on what's happening. Glasses, girl, and hurry!"

The flagon vanished, was replaced with another, more. Wine and conversation flowed and old battles were refought and old engagements remembered. Here, in this room, paid enemies faced each other and future foes sat and toasted each other in wine.

Gartok mentioned Craig.

"A bad world," said Chue Tung, his yellow skin gleaming like oiled leather in the dancing firelight. "Years ago now, six, seven, eight, maybe?"

"Does it matter?" A man a little more drunk than the rest, snapped his impatience. "Get on with it, man."

"Please," said another, quickly. "Eight years, you think?"

"Eight." Chue Tung looked at the one who had interrupted. One day they would meet and then revenge would be sweet. For now he would act the congenial spinner of reminiscences. "It was a small engagement, like yours, Kars, or so it started out to be. A simple police-job. I landed with a couple of hundred men and within a month we had the area pacified. All nice and neat—then the women took a hand. We lost fifteen men in three days and I'm not going to tell you how they died. We had a pretty tough commander at the time, Elque Imballa, anyone know him?" Pausing he looked at his listeners. "No? Well, he'd dead now but you could have served under worse. At least he took care of his own. Fifteen men had died so he took thirty locals and shot them. After that he took steps to end the danger."

Gartok was interested. "How?"

"The women were the trouble—you know how soldiers are when there's no prospect of action. Looting, raping, they do it all the time. There was nothing to loot so only one thing was left. Imballa had the entire area swept and all females assembled. Then he got the armorers to make some special undergarments for them to wear. Pants of wire mesh fitted with a friction bomb. They were safe until someone tried to jerk them off then—bang!" He made an expressive gesture.

"And?"

"A couple of fools tried it and ended up as mincemeat. After they had been buried the others learned the lesson. The women too. Try to get near them and they'd scream and go for your eyes. It wasn't much fun for anyone but it solved the problem. In his own way Elque Imballa was a pretty shrewd man."

For a long moment there was silence then a man said, dryly, "I'm not calling you a liar, Chue, but if anyone else had told me a story like that I'd be tempted to doubt his word."

"I'm glad that you're not calling me a liar, Amil," said Chue Tung softly. "I'd hate to kill you without getting paid for it."

Gartok, recognizing the undercurrent of hostility, said, "Talking of paying who is due to order the next flagon of wine?"

The talk moved on, took direction, revealed why each was present. Work was scarce and expenses high. The mines were waiting to swallow any who couldn't meet his debts. Times were hard for free-lance mercenaries.

"We need a good war," said one. "Something on a rich world with little fighting and guaranteed pay. That or a takeover. A bloodless victory with a long-term contract."

"I almost had it." The man was small, thin, his face gaunt, his eyes darting like restless birds. "The best prospect a man could ever hope to get. A friend passed me the word. He'd got a job training some retainers in the use of arms and from what he told me it was gravy all the way. Not much in the way of pay but the opportunity was there and the prospects were superb. I'd have been set for life."

"Talk," said a dour-faced man who sat in a corner. "We've heard it all before, Relldo."

"Maybe, but this time it's the truth. I told you the man was a friend. Well, to cut it short, I got to where he was working and found I'd arrived too late. Gnais was dead and so was the man who'd employed him. He was Lord Gydapen Prabang. His retainers were to start a war and conquer the entire damned planet. There would be no opposition. We'd all get rich. Then something happened and he got himself killed."

"How?" Gartok helped himself to more wine. "Accident?"

"Idiocy." Relldo scowled at his wine. "There was trouble between Gydapen and a woman, the Lady Lavinia Del Belamosk. She'd won the aide of a stranger—a man called Dumarest. He was a traveller, I think, a tall man who wore grey and carried a knife in his boot. He could be dead now but I doubt it. His sort are hard to kill."

"And?"

"He became involved and took a hand. He hit Gydapen with the woman and a few others in an attempt to steal the guns. At least I think that's the way it was. I wasn't there at the time, remember, but I learned what happened from a retainer who saw it all. Anyway, Gydapen gained the upper hand and then threw away his advantage. That's why I called him an idiot. He was tricked into allowing Dumarest to get a knife in his hands." Pausing Relldo added, slowly, "Could you believe that one man could kill another with a thrown knife when the victim had a laser in his hand aimed and ready to fire?"

"Is that what happened?"

"My informant saw it done."

"Fast," said Chue Tung before Gartok could comment. "A man who could do that would have to be fast."

"Damned fast," agreed Relldo. "And from what I was told Dumarest is all of that. When he moved it was like a blur, a flash of steel, a thud and Gydapen was falling with a knife in his throat. The next thing bullets were flying and that was the end of the war. My usual kind of luck—all of it bad. I was near stranded and had to travel Low."

He looked it; the loss of body-fat was a characteristic sign, tissue lost while he had lain doped, frozen and ninety per cent dead in a casket designed for the transportation of animals. Risking the fifteen percent death rate for the sake of cheap travel.

Chue Tung said, thoughtfully, "Maybe you left too soon. Something could have been arranged, perhaps. Where is this place?"

"A world on the edge of the Rift." Relldo scowled as he finished his wine. "But I would not have stayed even if Gnais had been alive. Not for long, anyway. Not once I'd seen the planet."

"Why not?"

"Because when I kill a man I like to know that he's dead. On Zakym that doesn't happen. The damned place is rotten with ghosts."

Chapter TWO

The woman standing against the parapet couldn't be real
for Dumarest had seen her lying dead on a world far distant in time and space and yet, as he watched, she smiled
at him and extended her hands and took a step closer
while the soft tones of her voice caressed his ears.

"Earl, it has been so long. Why must I continue to wait?
We should be together always. Have you forgotten how
close we were? How much in love? I was your wife, my
darling. Your wife!"

A ship-liaison, good only for as long as both wanted it,
a common practice among free traders especially those
risking the dangers of clouded space. For such men
pleasures were things to be taken and cherished and used
while the opportunity existed.

Yet it had been more than that. There had been love
and care and a tender regard.

"Earl!" Lallia lifted her hands and stepped toward him.
Against the sky her hair was a mass of shimmering ebon,
her skin smooth and firm over muscle and bone, her body
a remembered delight. "Earl?"

And then she was gone and, again, he was alone.

Leaning back in his chair Dumarest looked at the sky.
The twin suns filled the heavens of Zakym with violet and
magenta, the light merged now, the orbs close and low in
the azure bowl. Soon it would be night and darkness
would seal the land, but now the air held an oddly metallic taint and was still as though at the approach of a
storm.

There would be no storm. There would be nothing but
the darkness and another day would have passed as so
many had passed before it. And, in the meantime, the
dead reigned.

Delusia—the time when the dead walked and talked and communed with the living.

A planetary insanity of which he was a part.

If it was an insanity.

It was hard now to be sure. At first the explanation had been so obvious; wild radiation from the twin suns, merging as they closed, blasting space with energies which distorted the microcurrents of the brain and giving rise to hallucinations. Figments of memory made apparently real, words spoken but heard only by the one concerned, figures seen, advice taken, counsel asked. And yet he was a stranger, born and reared outside this culture and how could he be certain that of them all he alone was right?

"Earl!" Another figure standing where the other had been but this time one with hair of a somber red. Kalin? Always she seemed to be close but, as he rose he recognized the woman. Not Kalin but Dephine. Another who had claimed to have loved him and had played him false. Helping him even while she worked to destroy him by unconsciously leading him to the world on which he had found the spectrum of a forgotten sun. His sun. The one which warmed Earth. His world which, at last, he was certain he could find given time and money. "Do you still hate me, Earl?"

"Should I?"

"I intended to sell you to the Cyclan. You know that. My words, my acts, all were to hold you and waste time."

"Yes."

"And still you do not hate?"

She blurred as he made no answer, dissolving to change into another figure, thin, tall, haggard, the eyes accusing, the hands lifted as if to ward off a blow.

Chagney whom he had forced to breathe space.

"You killed me," he said. "You sent me into the void. I had done you no harm. Why did you kill me? Why didn't you listen?"

To the sound of crying, thin, remote—unforgettable!

Dumarest turned and looked over the inner wall of the parapet into the courtyard below. Retainers stood in the open space, some moving, talking as they walked, their faces animated as they watched and listen to people he could not see. Others, equally engrossed, spoke to relations long dead or to lovers and friends, companions and, even the children of their flesh who had succumbed.

Glancing at the sky he judged the position of the suns. This period of delusia had been strong but already the orbs were moving apart and soon it would be over.

"Earl!" Another woman but this time real. The Lady Lavinia Del Belamosk, tall, her hair a rippling waterfall of liquid midnight barred with silver, breasts prominent beneath the taut fabric of her blouse came toward him along the promenade. "Darling, I was worried. You have been sitting up here for so long."

"I was thinking."

"Of Earth?" Her smile was that of a mother to a child. "Your world. The planet of legend. Yes, I know," she said quickly as he frowned, "It is real. You are sure of that because you were born on it and all the rest of us have forgotten where it is to be found. As you have forgotten."

"No," he said. "I didn't forget. I never knew."

"Of course—what could a runaway boy know of spacial coordinates. And for years now you've been trying to find the way back. But, my darling, why should you bother now? You have me. You have what I own. And you have land of your own."

"No."

"Yes," she insisted. "The Council voted it. You can't refuse."

Land which was almost worthless in the sense that it couldn't be sold. And it took time to breed animals for fur and hides, to plant and harvest crops, to sift the upper layers for decorative stones and diluted minerals. The upper surface—below that the Sungari ruled. As they ruled at night. Sharing the world with men who owned the surface and the day.

Turning he again saw Dephine, tall, her eyes mocking, metallic glints reflected from the metal tipping her fingers. The attribute of a harlot and yet she had been a member of a family cursed with pride. Perhaps he had offered her an escape from the iron bonds of ancient tradition. Or it could have been simply that he had been prey for her predator-like instinct.

It didn't matter now. Dephine was dead. Only on Zakym did she return to haunt him with her enigmatic smile and memories of what might have been. But the threat of the Cyclan remained. The reason why he had run from Harald. The reason why he was here, in this castle, with this woman, on this peculiar world.

"Earl?" Lavinia was concerned. "Earl, are you well?"

He stared at her, wondering for a moment if she were real or merely another delusion. Wondering too why she appeared to be unaffected by the delusia and why he seemed to be more susceptible of late. Was instinct urging him to escape while he had the chance? Primitive caution overriding logical consideration and striving for attention by this peculiar distortion of his senses?

"Earl?"

"It's nothing."

Stepping forward she lifted her hand and gently ran her fingers through his hair. Beneath their tips she could feel the line of freshly healed tissue running over the scalp. Gydapen's last, wild shot had found a target, the beam of the laser searing almost to the bone. Could such a wound have unexpected aftereffects?

Guessing her thoughts he said, impatiently, "I'm all right, Lavinia. There's nothing wrong with me."

Then why did he turn and thrash in his sleep? Even when lying in her arms she was conscious of his tension, his inner turmoil. A product of the jungle, she thought, looking at him. Not the place of trees and underbrush, or the hunted and hunters to be found in tropic places but the harsher, bleaker jungle to be found among the stars where it was a matter of each man for himself and mercy was, like charity, a meaningless word.

How often had he killed? Did he now, at times of delusia, see again those faces he had known betraying the shock of death finally realized. Did enemies come to taunt and foes to plead? In his lonely vigils on the promenade did he talk again to those he had loved and who had loved him?

Only the dead returned at such times and it was foolish to be jealous of the dead but, at times, Lavinia wished she could see them, talk with them, warn them to stay clear of her man.

As Charles stayed clear. As Bertram. As Hulong and others she had loved and who had known her body. Now,

for her, for always, there could be only one man in her
life. One potential father of her children.

"Earl!"

He was looking over the parapet to where a dark fleck
showed as a deeper mote against the sky. A raft which
came closer, taking shape and form, revealing the figures
riding in the open body of the vehicle. They were too far
to distinguish but Lavinia had no doubt as to their identity.

"Our friends, Earl. Coming from town. I told you I had
invited them to dinner."

They had left it late. As the raft came in to settle in the
courtyard the sky was deepening to a rich purple, the horizon barely tinged with the fading glow of sunset.

"We'd best go down, darling." Lavania slipped her hand
through the curve of Dumarest's arm. "Soon it will be curfew."

It sounded as he lay soaking in a bath of steaming
water the deep, sonorous throbbing giving rise to sympa-
thetic tintinnabulations so that the vases with their con-
tents of scented crystals, the carved ornaments of stone,
the suspended cascades of engraved glass all became chim-
ing bells. Dumarest ducked, feeling water close his ears,
waiting until his chest ached with the need of air, rising to
blow and to hear the final throb of curfew as it sent
echoes resonating from the walls, the very structure of the
castle.

Already the building would have been sealed. Covers
closed the air-shafts, the doors leading into the open were
locked and guarded, the courtyard would be deserted.
Only within the building itself would there be signs of life
and all movement would be through connecting chambers
or tunnels gouged from the upper regions of the soil. In
town it would be the same. In every building now in
darkness the curfew would have sounded and the Pact
obeyed.

From sunset to sunrise the Sungari ruled without question.

Water splashed as Dumarest rose from the bath, running in little rivulets over his shoulders, the hard planes of
torso and stomach, the columns of his thighs. The flesh of

his upper body was traced with the thin lines of old scars; wounds delivered with a naked blade which he had taken when young and when to fight in the ring was the only way in which to earn a living. Standing, remembering, he heard again the roar of the watching crowd, the animal-like baying as men and women leaned forward avid for the sight of blood and pain and wounds and death.

"Earl?"

He ignored the call, looking into a mirror, nostrils filled with the odor of perfumes. Now it was that of flowers and rare spices, then it had been the raw taint of oil and sweat and fear, the sickly sweetness of blood, the stench of vomit and excreta voided at the approach of death.

Here, now, there was none of that. In this place was softness and comfort and servile retainers to do his bidding. There was good food and wine and scented baths. There was a woman who loved him and a life which many would envy. A good exchange, perhaps, for a life of endless movement. Of privation and danger and the constant threat of conflict. Even the sacrifice of his search for Earth was a small price to pay for the comfort he now enjoyed. He had found a refuge, a haven, and if it was one of darkness well, what of that? A man could learn to do without sight of the stars. He could learn to live only for the day and to yield the night to another race.

"Earl!" Lavania called again, her voice impatient. "Hurry, darling. Our guests will be waiting."

"Let them wait."

"What?"

"Nothing."

To quarrel would be foolish and what reason did he have for irritation? The figures which had come to him on the upper promenade, perhaps? The dead who had returned to smile and talk and to waken old memories. To rip the protective scabs from old wounds. And Chagney—always there was Chagney and, always, there was the sound of the thin, remote crying.

The crying.

The endless crying!

"Earl—"

He felt the touch on his shoulder and moved, springing to one side, one hand snatching up a tall, slender container of astringent liquid, sending it to smash against the wall, the jagged remains lifting like a dagger as his free hand swung like a blunted sword.

He saw the face before it landed, the eyes wide with shock, the parted lips, the dawn of terror and pulled back the stiffened palm so that only the tips of the fingers caught the fabric of her robe. It ripped, ripped again as the jagged glass, diverted, fretted the material from shoulder to waist.

"Earl! For God's sake!"

Lavinia recoiled, one hand rising to her mouth, the fingers trembling, betraying her fear. A foot, as bare as the body which showed through the ruined garment, slipped on a wet patch and she staggered and almost fell. Would have fallen had not Dumarest caught her arm.

"No! Don't! You——are you mad?"

Releasing her he watched as she stepped back against the wall. Fear had blanched her cheeks and robbed her lungs of air so that now she gasped, the proud breasts rising, the mane of hair darker by contrast.

Then, as he made no move toward her, she said, "Why, Earl? Why?"

"You touched me. I was thinking and, well, you startled me."

"And for that you would have killed me?"

"No."

"Don't lie! I saw it in your face, your eyes. They belonged to an animal. You were a creature determined to kill."

"Not you, Lavinia."

"Who else was here?"

Memories, a reminder, a peril which always threatened. The robe she wore was the color of flame. He had caught a glimpse of scarlet, a hint of motion, had felt the touch and had reacted without conscious thought. But how to explain?

"You were wearing red," he said. "I'm sensitive to that color. It has certain unpleasant associations."

"I'll burn everything red I own!"

"No, the color suits you." He smiled and, reaching out, lifted a portion of the garment and let it slip through his fingers. "I'm just trying to make you understand. I meant

you no harm—surely you know that? It was just that I was
thinking and you touched me and old habits took over."

"Old?" Lavinia shook her head. "Not old, Earl. Time
blunts the speed of reflexes and your's are the fastest I've
ever seen. You would have killed me if you hadn't recognized me in time. An ordinary man would have been un-
able to stop. An assassin would be dead. How could
anyone stand against you?" She looked down at her ruined
garment and then, with eyes still lowered, said, quietly,
"Who did I remind you of, Earl?"

"No one." The truth—the enemy wore no particular
face. "It was an accident, Lavinia. Let's forget it."

"Something is worrying you. I've felt it for some time
now. But what, my darling? You are safe here. No enemy can reach you. My retainers will protect you in case
of need. Earl—trust me!"

She was a woman and her intuition was strong but to
trust her was to put a knife in her hand to hold against his
throat.

He said, "Forget it, Lavinia. Please."

"But—"

"Please!"

He closed the distance between them and took her in
his arms, holding her close, feeling the warm softness of
her flesh against his own, the soft yielding of her breasts,
the firm curves of hips and thighs. A good way to distract
a woman and she was a creature made for love.

"Earl!"

She stirred in his arms, straining, her perfume filling his
nostrils with the scent of expensive distillations, the odor
mingling with her natural exudations; the subtle smells of
her hair, the animal-scent of her femininity. Triggers which
stimulated his maleness and worked their ancient, biological magic.

"Darling!" His proximity, his need, fired her response.
She threw back her head, face misted with passion, hands
rising to clasp his neck. The heat of her body matched the
color of her robe. "Earl, my darling! My love! My love!"

Dinner was late that evening but, once started,
progresses as usual when guests were present at Castle Be-
lemosk. A succession of dishes accompanied by appro-

priate wines together with compotes, nuts, fruits, sweetmeats, comfits—items to titivate the palate and to stretch the occasion as did the entertainers. Dumarest crushed a nut between his palms and watched as a trio of young girls danced with lithe grace, making up in natural beauty what they lacked in trained skill. Before them an old man had chanted a saga, before him a juggler had kept glittering balls dancing through the air. He had followed a harpist and the girls would be followed by a man skilled on a flute.

"Lavinia, my dear, always your hospitality is superb!" Fhard Erason, hard, blocky, a member of the Council of Zakym, leaned back in his chair as a servant refilled his goblet. His face was flushed a little and his eyes held a glitter but he was far from drunk. "At times I envy you and, always, I envy the man at your side."

A little more and there would have been grounds for a quarrel, for weapons at dawn and injury or death waiting one or both. Crushing another nut Dumarest wondered if the baiting had been deliberate but the man had ended in time and left the comment as a compliment. And yet, if he had added 'no matter who he might be' what then?

"A fine chef, skilled entertainers, a magnificent selection of wines—what more could any man want?" Alacorus, gruffly polite yet a little clumsy in his choice of words. He, like Howich Suchong, like Navalok, like the Lord Roland Acrae also belonged to the Council. An accident that so many should have gathered at this time?

A triple beat signalled the ending of the dancers' performance. It was followed by a scatter of applause and the ringing jingle of thrown coins. Flushing the girls picked up their reward and ran with a flash of silken limbs from the platform. The flutist, tall, thin, his hands like those of a woman, took his place, coughed, waited a moment then began to play.

From his place at Lavinia's left hand Roland said, "Lavinia, my dear, you are looking positively radiant."

Her smile was enigmatic.

"You have blossomed since Dumarest came." The glass he held was of fragile glass fitted with a delicate stem. He looked down at it, now snapped, a thin smear of blood on one finger. "I—. My apologies, Lavinia, how did that happen?"

"An accident, as you say." Imperiously she gestured to a servant to provide a replacement. "Your hand?"

"It is nothing." He sucked at the minor wound, his eyes searching her face, the mane of her hair now held in a silver mesh sparkling with gems. "Are you happy, my dear?"

"Roland—how can you doubt?" She turned to him, lips moistly parted, the gleam of white teeth showing between the scarlet. "I never thought I would ever know such fulfillment. Earl is a man! With him at my side—"

"If he stays, my dear."

"If he stays," she admitted, and a shadow misted her eyes. It lasted a moment then was gone. "He will stay," she said. "And together we shall rule. His lands and mine together." She saw his momentary frown. "Roland? Is something wrong?"

"Later, my dear. It is nothing but—well, later. We have plenty of time."

The entire night if necessary—once trapped by the darkness none could leave. Until dawn each would do as he wished to beguile the tedium. There would be talk, more wine, sweetmeats, mutual entertainments and, finally, sleep. And, at dawn, freed of the prison of the night, life would begin again.

The flutist finished his piece, offered to play another, was refused and stalked from the hall. The table was cleared, the servants making a final survey before they left to enjoy their own repast and, within minutes, Lavinia and her guests were alone.

"A good meal." Navalok rose and stretched and took a few steps to where a fire glowed in a heap of embers on a dulled platform of stone. He held his hands to it for a moment, enjoying the sight, the comfort of the flame, then turned. "The dish of broiled meat dusted with nuts and spiced with that pungent sauce. The one adorned with the head of a stallion in pastry."

"You want the recipe?" Lavinia smiled at his nod. "You shall have it if I have to torment the cook to obtain it. A friend like yourself can be denied nothing."

An offer with qualifications unnecessary to stipulate as he knew. And yet, if he had been younger, perhaps . . .

As if reading his mind Roland said, quietly, "Think of your youth, Navalok. If you had been the consort of such a woman would you have been gentle to those who hoped to gain what you held?"

"No."

"Then—"

"Spare me your warnings, Roland. I am not wholly a fool." Novalok glanced to where Dumarest stood beyond the table. In the somber glow he looked ghost-like in the plainness of his clothing. A man who wore no gems and who scorned the slightest decoration.

Was there a reason?

Navalok studied the clothing. The tunic was high around the throat, the sleeves long and snug at the wrists, the hem falling to mid-thigh. Pants of the same material were thrust into knee-high boots and the hilt of a knife rose above the right. A man who looked what he was, he decided. A traveller, a fighter, a man who walked alone.

"Grey," mused Navalok. "Why does he wear grey?"

"Camouflage, perhaps?" Roland ventured a guess. "Bright colors could offend as well as attract possibly unwelcome attention. Habit? A cultural conditioning? There could be many explanations but I think the obvious is the answer. We tend to forget that, for some, clothing is a matter of functional necessity and not of stylish fashion. For a man on the move, needing to carry little, his garments must be both tough and efficient."

"But now that he is living here in the castle?" Navalok glanced to where Lavinia was deep in conversation with Suchong. "Why now?"

"Habit."

"But surely, now he's with Lavinia—"

"Habit," said Roland again, quickly. The man was treading on dangerous ground. As a relative of the woman's he would be forced to demand an apology if a slur was made and this was no time to create discord. "Let us join the others," he suggested. "We don't want to appear indifferent."

Dumarest watched as they moved over the tesselated floor. Navalok was old, Roland younger but still far Lavinia's senior. A curse with which he had to live as did all men born out of their time. From the first Dumarest had recognized the affection the man held for the woman, the hopeless yearning which he had learned to master and conceal. Yet there were times when he betrayed himself as when he had broken the glass.

A small thing, but had others noticed? And would it matter if they had?

Did anything really matter on this strange world where the dead walked when the suns were close and aliens ruled the night?

Lavinia smiled as she came toward him, resting one hand lightly on his arm, the fingers closing with a trace of possession.

"Earl, darling, you seem a little detached. Come and join the company. Alcorus has news."

He was talking about another member of the Council—gossip, not news, but on Zakym the two were often confused.

"I tried to bring Khaya along but you know how he is. That's why we were late. We did out best but he simply wasn't interested. Too busy with his worms, I imagine, and you know how much he hates to be disturbed."

"Worms!" Lavinia shook her head, laughing. "I've known Khaya Taiyuah all my life and still I don't understand him. What pleasure can he possibly find in such an odd hobby?"

"It isn't exactly a hobby," protested Roland. "He's trying to breed a new strain of silkworm. It could have wide commercial application if he succeeds."

"If!" Lavinia shrugged. "A small word with a big meaning. If we had wings we could fly. If sand was gold we'd all be rich. What do you think, Alcorus?"

She wasn't interested, Dumarest knew, but was doing a good job of lightening the atmosphere. Alcorus didn't help.

"I have no opinion."

"Howich?"

Suchong grunted as he sipped his wine. "The man is too old. He could be growing senile. I know we have no right to scorn his interest, but it is more than that. How often does he attend Council? And he forgets his manners. Why, when we visited, he didn't even greet us. All we were given was a message that he was not to be disturbed. How could we argue? A man is master in his own house."

If the man happened to be a lord of Zakym and not a servant or artisan or a visitor from another world.

Dumarest tasted bitterness and lifted a goblet from where it stood among others, filling it with wine from a decanter, swallowing the liquid and feeling warmth spread from it down his throat and into his stomach.

It didn't help.

He needed money, not wine. He needed the coordinates of Earth and a ship to carry him across the void. He wanted to get back home.

Chapter THREE

The talk was a fountain; words kept spinning as the juggler had maintained his gilded orbs in the air without apparent effort. An attribute of those who were accustomed to the long, leisurely discussions of the night, but beneath the talk of weather, or crops and herds, of relationships and recipes, entertainers, exchanges, there was an undertone of something else. Navalok edged toward it.

"This should be a good season for you, Lavinia. I saw your herd in the Iron Mountains a few days ago. They look prime beasts in every way. Good, strong foals which should interest the buyers when they arrive."

"One already has." Suchong leaned forward in his chair to better inhale the plume of scented smoke rising in an amber thread from a container of gemmed silver. "I met him in town. A buyer from beyond the Rift coming early so as to make a good selection. I wonder he hasn't contacted you."

"He will if he's interested in mounts," she said. "From where? Beyond the Rift, I know, but which world?"

"Tyumen, I think. Or was it Tyrahmen?" Suchong lifted his head. His face, wreathed by the smoke, was almost saffron and his eyes held a peculiar glitter. "His name is Mbom Chelhar and he seems to have money. The best chamber at the hotel, the best foods and wines. He wears jewels on each finger and smells of riches. An agent, I think, for some wealthy ruler or a combine. We talked about my freshendi and, if the crop is as good as I think it will be, then I shall be a happy man."

"And if not?" Fhard Erason answered his own question. "We plant again and hope and wait again and, while we wait, try not to envy others. But you, Lavinia, have nothing to worry you. As Navalok mentioned your herd is a

32

certain source of revenue. If my lands grew the herbs they need I too would breed such animals." And then he added, with apparent casualness, "Gydapen was a fool not to have diversified more than he did. The desert could have been put to better use."

Lavinia said, sharply, "Gydapen is dead."

"But his son is not." Alcorus looked from one to the other. "Yes, he had a son, a boy born to a woman he married while travelling off-world. A secret he kept from all but a few. The lad would be grown now and there is talk of his claiming his inheritance."

"What inheritance?" Lavinia looked at Suchong, at Navalok. "The lands were taken and voted to Earl. It was a Council decision."

"And perhaps a wrong one." Navalok was blunt. "We were confused, disturbed, unsure of our facts and you were pressing. The land needed an owner—retainers must be aware of a firm hand, but we could have made a mistake. And, naturally, we knew nothing of Gydapen's son."

"If he is his son."

"The facts are attested."

"But—" She broke off, aware of her position. Gydapen had promised her marriage and, even for reasons of his own, would have fulfilled the pledge had she permitted it. The previous marriage meant nothing—her own would have taken precedence and her children would have been the undoubted heirs. But to mention it. To remind those present that she had believed everything he told her. To admit that she had been little better than a gullible fool!

Dumarest said, "This talk of Gydapen's early marriage. When did it begin?"

"Recently. Why?"

"Who mentioned it? Who spread the rumor?" He looked at the blank faces. "Roland?"

"I don't know, Earl," he confessed. "I heard it from Jmombota. He claimed nothing for it but said that it was common knowledge. I think he wanted me to relay the news. There was no need. Three others asked me about it within two days and then—" He broke off, shoulders lifting in a helpless gesture. "Perhaps we should talk about it."

"About what?" Lavinia blazed her anger. "Gydapen was

a dangerous man. If it hadn't been for Earl all of you would now be paying him homage. Is this how you thank the man who saved you?"

"Please, Lavinia." Navalok made a soothing gesture. "Don't upset yourself."

"Are you mad?" She stared at the others. "Are you all mad? Gydapen—"

"Is dead as you mentioned, my dear," said Erason a little impatiently. "We all know that."

"And you know what he intended. He threatened our safety. He would have broken the Pact or—"

Again Erason interrupted.

"We aren't sure of that, Lavinia. In fact we are sure of very little. Gydapen had guns, that is true. He was training his retainers to use them, that also is true. He had hired a mercenary, Gnais, to instill obedience and elementary drill. Gnais is dead and so is Gydapen. These things we know. But other things are less clear. Gydapen wanted to extend his mining operations. He told us that. A danger to the Pact, I admit, and also I admit we were concerned as to what action the Sungari would take once it had been broken. But the Pact wasn't broken and so the problem did not arise. What have we left? An accusation, made by you, that Gydapen intended a war of conquest."

"An accusation made not only by Lavinia," said Roland, quickly. "I made it also."

"And you are a part of her Family." Navalok did not elaborate, it was unnecessary, a man would lie for a relative and more than lie for a woman he loved. "And you could both be speaking the truth as you know it. In fact we all are convinced of that." Pausing he added, softly, "It was a pity Gydapen was killed. Dead he can answer no questions."

"And present no threat." Lavinia drew in her breath, making an obvious effort to master her anger. "What is happening here? If you are not all mad then what rewards have been offered for you to blind yourselves to truth? How high did you set your honor?"

Suchong said, thickly, "Woman, you dare to smear my name and that of my Family? If you were a man—"

"If?" Her contempt was a blow. "Don't let that stop you

my Lord of Suchong. At dawn? On the upper promenade?"

"You bitch! You—"

"Are overheated," said Dumarest. "And this has gone
far enough."

He dominated them with his presence, his height, the
aura which radiated from his somber figure. Despite their
talk and wild threats the rulers of Zakym were strangers to
violence as he knew it. They adhered to the punctilious
code of the duello—he killed in order to survive and to
give an opponent a chance was to act the fool. Looking at
him Lavinia remembered that, remembered too how close
he had come to killing her. A fraction less swift in his
recognition and her larynx would have been crushed, the
splinters of glass thrust up beneath her lower ribs into
heart and lung.

Drugged by his smoke Suchong had found unsuspected
courage.

"You," he said, thinly. "Who are you to give us orders?
A stranger. A fighter and little more. On Zakym we
treasure the old ways and the old blood. We have no time
for those who do not belong!"

He would die, Lavinia was certain of it. Dumarest
would stoop and rise and his knife would flash as she had
seen it flash before and Suchong would double, the steel
buried in his heart and the insult would be avenged.

Instead he laughed.

It was a sound divorced from humor, the snarl of a
beast, the bared teeth and exhalation a sound more stinging than the lash of a whip. It held contempt and an acid
comment on their concept of honor. It showed the hol-
lowness of gratitude. It made them feel soiled and a little
ridiculous and more than a little ashamed.

Then he said, bluntly, "You want to get rid of me, is
that it?"

"No, Earl! No!"

He ignored the woman, looking at Roland, seeing the
answer in his eyes, at the others, seeing the same thing.
Roland, at least, was honest, his desire was born in human, natural jealousy and desire. Once Dumarest had
gone Lavinia might remember him. Could even turn to

him. If she did he would consider honor spent wisely for the sake of realized ambition.

The others?

Suchong had spoken the truth. He was an outsider. He was a stranger. Zenophobia, incredible in this age, was not dead. And, on small, backward worlds like Zakym, what place had someone who did not belong?

"I own land on this world," said Dumarest, quietly. "Gydapen's estate. I didn't ask for it—you voted that it should be given to me. But I think I earned it. No matter what you say or pretend to believe you know the danger he represented. Well, he is dead now and can do no harm. And you have had time to regret what you did. And you talk of a mysterious son of his who claims to be the natural heir."

"An attested claim, Earl," said Roland. "The ceremony of marriage was performed by a monk of the Church of Universal Brotherhood. The birth of the child, the acknowledged parents, the witnesses—there can be no argument."

And no real proof if it came down to it. The original child could have died, the present claimant an impostor, but Dumarest didn't mention what should have been obvious to all. It suited them to believe and, should the new owner prove intractable, ways could be devised to eliminate him once the future of the land had been decided.

Roland said, slowly, "I don't like this, Earl. It wasn't my decision. I think you have earned all that has been given you. I know I would be pleased for you to stay among us."

"He will stay," said Lavinia. "Listen to me, all of you! Dumarest will stay!"

He wondered what made her so sure.

What made him so eager to go.

Satiation, perhaps. Life was cloying with its ease and he sensed he was in a trap baited with honey and entrancing perfume. The softness of her body, the warmth of her bed, the future she spoke of so often, the hints, the acceptance that, no matter what he decided, she would get her own way. And the other thing. The pressure at the base of his skull. The odd feeling of detachment. The sudden wakings in the night, the fear, the imagined sound of crying.

Crying.

The ghosts.

The lost and lonely ghosts.

Dumarest blinked and looked sharply around but the figures he had imagined vanished as he concentrated. Tricks of the light and not of delusia. The suns were far on their journey by now, the sky dark aside from the glitter of stars, cold and remote points glittering like gems against the bowl of the heavens. There would be sheets and curtains of luminescence, the fuzz of distant nebulae, the somber blotches of interstellar dust. The Rift would be close, stars set close yet masked by the ochre haze of dust, a pass through a host of suns into the empty spaces beyond.

Did Sungari study the heavens?

Did they check and count and look, perhaps, for their home world? If they had a home world. If they had eyes. If they cared.

"Earl?" Lavinia was looking at him. They were all looking at him and Dumarest realized that he had been standing silent and ominous. The woman had expected an answer. She was still expecting it. But to what? A statement of some kind? A challenge?

She said, "Earl, tell them you will stay."

That wasn't the problem. To the watching faces he said, "You gave me land. I will not allow it to be taken from me. But I am willing to sell it."

"Sell it?" Navalok hadn't considered the possibility. Now he stood, frowning. "For how much?"

"Have it valued. I will take one quarter of the estimate in cash. Each of the Council can contribute to the total. How you determine how much each should give I leave to you."

"Money," said Suchong. Amber smoke wreathed his face, clung in tendrils to his hair. "I was right—how can we trust a stranger who is willing to sell his land."

"It would restore the old blood," said Erason. "And it is a solution."

"Earl is being kind." This from Alcorus. "It can't be easy for him."

"And it won't be easy for us," said Roland. He pulled thoughtfully at his left ear. "How can we put a price on

Gydapen's estate? When we trade land we do it by exchange or barter and always in small parcels. When did we ever sell an entire estate? When would anyone ever be permitted to buy? It will take time. And the claimant—will he be willing to wait?"

"He has no choice." Navalok shrugged. "Personally I've finished with the matter. What needed to be said has been spoken. An arrangement has been made and one I think fair to all. It is time now to share wine and end our differences. We are of the Council of Zakym. Let us remember our dignity."

Suchong said, suspiciously, "Are you hinting that I have conducted myself with less than proper standing?"

"No."

"I am old and need more help than most but, if you smear my name, then I must demand satisfaction." The smoke had made him first aggressive then maudlin. Tears shone in his glittering eyes. "Satisfaction," he repeated. "On the upper promenade at dawn. Knives, I think. I used to be good with a knife when I was young."

"I know," said Alcorus. "We were all good when young. It isn't kind of you to remind us." Then, turning toward the woman, his tone became formal. "Lady Lavinia Del Belamosk, for any friction caused while beneath your roof as your guests we apologize. Let all hurtful words be as never uttered. Let all misunderstanding be swept away. Let friendship prevail. This, of your kindness, we beg."

A ritual born of the long nights and incompatible company when hot words, unforgiven, could lead to life-long enmity. One she completed with equal stiffness.

"As my guests you are welcome now and in the future. Friendship prevails. This, of your kindness, I beg."

Then, as they sipped the ceremonial toast she whispered, "Earl! I'm sick of these fools! Take me to bed!"

It was a wide and ornate couch set in a chamber touched with brightness; inset panes reflecting the light of golden lanterns in shimmers of ruby and yellow, violet and blue, amber, purple, cerise, magenta. Broken rainbows spilled from clusters of glass, the pendants scored with fine, diffracting lines. A doll dressed as a bride sat on a stool and watched with emerald eyes. In vases of striated marble flowers scented the air, thick, fleshy petals bearing swirls of gold on scarlet, their stamens a somber black. A container held glimmering liquid in which bubbles rose in a constant stream to burst in thin, brittle tinklings. A clock counted the hours.

"Idiots!" Lavinia kicked at a cushion and sent it flying to strike a table and send glasses flying. As they shattered she sent a vase to splinter against a wall. "The fools! Are they mad? Have they no memory? Earl, for my people, I apologize. As for the Council—"

Dumarest caught her arm as she was about to add to the destruction.

"That's enough."

"Release me!"

"Stop acting like a spoiled child!" His eyes met hers, held them, watched as the fury died. "That's better. Why destroy things which have done you no harm?"

"Why allow men to live who have insulted you so deeply?"

"Should I have killed them for speaking their minds?"

"You gave in too easily," she snapped. "Any man worthy of the man will fight to hold his own. You should have defied them. What could they do if you had?"

Dryly he said, "Do? They could kill me, Lavinia. From the shadows, from behind, with poison or disease or sabotage. With an assassin or someone eager to earn a reward. No man can withstand a group determined on his death."

The answer of a coward? From another she might have thought so but she knew that Dumarest had no lack of courage. Even while they had talked he must have been assessing the situation, gauging probabilities and deciding on a course of action. But what?

"Defying them would have gained nothing," he said when she asked the question. "But you heard what Roland said—first the estate must be valued and then the money to pay me must be found. All of it will take time."

Time! The answer, of course, one she had been too blind to see. Time in which to prepare, to arrange support, to plan. Time in which he would be safe from the drives of impatient men.

"You tricked them," she said. "You guided them and

the fools couldn't see it. Earl, my darling, I didn't understand. Forgive me."

The clock hummed, gave a soft series of chimes, a peal of bells as if wafted from a temple on some distant shore. Colors flowed over the dial in a swathe of kaleidoscopic illumination which revealed bizarre figures moving in silhouette across the surface in a stately saraband.

Another hour gone—how many more until the dawn?

Dumarest crossed to the table disturbed by the flying cushion and, from the wreckage, selected an unbroken glass. His mouth felt dry and his head ached with a dull throbbing which ran from nape to temples. A bathroom opened from the chamber and he filled the glass with water, sipped, swallowed, then thrust his head beneath the faucet.

"Earl?" Lavinia watched him, her eyes anxious as he straightened, water dripping from his hair. He dried it with the towel she handed him and dug his fingers into the bunched muscles at the base of his skull. It didn't help. "That headache again? I've some drugs which could help."

Simple compounds which did nothing but raise the pain-level but they would help. He swallowed a triple dose, took water to wash down the tablets, drank more to ease his thirst.

As he set down the empty glass he said, "You and Roland are close. Has he mentioned anything about Gydapen's heir before?"

"No."

"Would he have done so had he known?"

"Yes—I am certain of it. We are friends, Earl. He has known me all my life and is of the Family. Had anything threatened me he would have spoken."

"This doesn't threaten you."

"It threatens you, Earl, and Roland knows what you mean to me. For him it would be the same." Pausing she added, thoughtfully. "There's something wrong, isn't there? Something which doesn't quite add up. You think there's more to this than just a son eager to regain his father's estate?"

"If he is the son."

"You think he isn't?"

"I'm not sure. Things could be as they seem or a cover

for something else. Gydapen had a plan to conquer this world. With armed men at his command he would have had little opposition. Mercenaries could have been hired to back his own retainers and, with the advantage of surprise, he would have won. But did he think of the plan all by himself? Was he working wholly alone. We know that he must have had at least one friend here on Zakym."

"The one who warned him we were coming to attack?"

"He was waiting for you," Dumarest reminded. "How else would he have known."

A warning which had almost cost them their lives and would have done had it not been for Dumarest's quick thinking and fantastic speed. He had said nothing more of it at the time—had he intended to leave? If so then what would be the problems of a backward world to him?

"A member of the Council," she said, bleakly. "Or someone close enough to one to know what was doing on. It could have been a friendly warning, Earl. We had time to fully explain. Whoever it was needn't have believed us."

"Perhaps," he admitted. "But there's something else. Gydapen had travelled off-world. Maybe he met someone, arranged something. Those guns we took had to be paid for. Mercenaries, if hired, don't work for nothing. There's little money on this world. Gydapen must have stripped himself to set up the operation and have promised rich rewards. Treasures, perhaps."

"Treasure?" Her laugh was brittle. "On Zakym?"

"The promise would have been enough. A handful of gems shown with the lie they had been won from the Sungari. A hint that there could be a mountain more waiting to be gained. I've known men to fight like demons for less."

And with relatively few estates manned by retainers softened by routine and a protected life, with few weapons and all strangers to violence as practiced by men accustomed to war the end was predictable. Some killings. Some attacks and destruction. A few carefully calculated atrocities and, like an overripe fruit, the planet would have fallen.

"Tremendous returns for a small investment," said Lavinia, bitterly. "A culture developed over centuries destroyed for the sake of money. Gydapen must have been insane. But, Earl, if he did have a partner then—"

"He would still be interested," said Dumarest. "The more so now that he doesn't have to share. But first he must obtain Gydapen's estate in order to have a base. The retainers will form a cadre of reliable men, a bodyguard he can trust. The new owner will provide a source of information and a means to exert pressure on the Council. He can't be the partner—he is too young for that. He must be a willing tool agreeable to being manipulated. But once established—"

"It will be the end of Zakym as we know it. The estates gone. The land ravaged. Slavery, maybe, everything that is vile. No! It mustn't be!"

Dumarest said, "Of course I could be wrong. It is only a guess."

"No," she said flatly. "You aren't wrong. It makes too much sense and it explains too much. But how to get the Council to believe it? They will think you are fighting to retain the estate. Earl—what can we do?"

"Nothing until dawn."

"Of course, but then?" She came toward him, hands lifting toward his shoulders, her eyes misted with appeal. "Do we fight?"

A touch, the pressure of her body, the appeal in her eyes—did she think it enough to make the problem his? Once he had the money all space was waiting and let those fight who had something to fight for. Why should he defend those who had made it plain he was unwanted among their company?

"We will fight," she said, flatly. "And you will help, Earl, you have no choice. Or do you care nothing for the future of our child?"

Chapter FOUR

It had grown colder and, as always at the onset of winter, the church was filled both with suppliants and those who simply desired to gain a little warmth and comfort. Both were welcome for who could tell when a word, a nod or smile, might not change a man from the path of violence? And, on Ilyard, such small victories were gains indeed. But this was a special occasion. Today Brother Eldon would burn.

The service would be short as these things always were. A man had died, leaving his body to commence the final journey into the infinite, and what he had left was nothing of real importance. It would be disposed of; a mass of decaying tissue fed to the cleansing flames, the ashes to be scattered so that, even in death, he would continue to serve as fertilizer if as nothing else.

And yet it was hard to think of the old monk as a heap of corruption.

Harder still to accept that never again would he be close at hand to help, to guide and advise, to lend his strength, to understand.

A loss which Brother Veac felt as he stood beside the door watching those assembled in the hall. Their smell rose from the benches to cling to the ceiling and walls; an odor of sweat and rancid oil, of dirt and natural exudations, of fear and privation. The stench of sickness, the reek of poverty. Yet not all were poor.

Among the crowd could be seen the flash of expensive fabrics, the gleam of gems, the sheen of rich cloaks. Men and women both who had cause to hold the dead monk in high regard and who had come to pay their last respects. Others too, hard men, one in particular with a flat, scarred face. A mercenary by the look of him and, as such, hardly a man to follow the Church.

"Kars Gartok," said a voice at his side. "I saw him enter."

Brother Biul, demonstrating again his seeming ability to read minds. He smiled as his companion turned.

"I noticed your interest—one I share. Why should a professional killer attend the last rites of an old monk? A mystery, brother, but one which will have to wait for a solution. It is time we began."

There were words, ceremonies deliberately kept devoid of mysticism, the throb of bells. Always there were bells, deep, musical notes captured on recorders, now filling the air with the melody gained on Hope where tremendous castings of bronze, silver and brass throbbed and droned with a solemn pulse which touched the wells of life itself. Here, in this place, with damp mottling the walls and the floor little more than tamped clay covered with tough but bleak matting, the sound was that of an outstretched hand closing in warm friendship.

Veac felt his eyes sting with tears.

It was the pain of personal loss and yet a little more than that. A man had been born, had chosen, had lived to spend his years in the service of others. He had suffered willingly and without complaint. He had helped and asked for nothing and, in return, murder had come to him in the guise of a plea for aid.

Who could have wanted the old man dead?

The tears streamed as the doors opened and flame showed waiting to embrace the small, withered figure on the bier. Veac let them fall, unashamed of his display of emotion and he was not alone. In the body of the hall a woman cried out and tore at her hair. A man called something, a farewell, in a tone gruff with anguish. Even the scarred mercenary lifted a hand and snapped a military salute, lowering his palm only after the doors had closed and the small body vanished from sight.

Veac stepped before him as Kars Gartok made his way toward the door.

"A moment, brother, if you would be so kind."

"I have time, brother." Gartok took two steps to one side, watching as a woman, heavily veiled, shoulders bowed and a handkerchief held to her eyes stumbled past. The man with her, rich in his puffed and pleated tunic, his cloak thick and lined with scarlet material, looked over her head at the monk.

"Later, brother, I shall return for audience. Such a man as that must not be forgotten. An extension, perhaps? Some little thing to remind those who come later what we have lost today?"

"You are most kind, brother." Veac was genuine in his response. "Brother Eldon will be missed but his work—the work of the Church—must continue."

"Of course. Of course." The man nodded, one hand on the arm of the woman. "I know the Church does not encourage personal enhancement—the whole embraces the part—but I have a personal regard and, well, later we shall speak of it. I will send word. Now, my dear, be brave. Soon we shall be home."

The mercenary drew in his breath as the couple moved on their way.

"Charl Embris," he murmured. "And his lady Othurine. He's rich enough to build you a Church of marble faced with gold. What did he owe the monk, I wonder? What service had he performed?" One he would never know, the Church retained its secrets, but the sight of the man emphasized the power which could be used to aid the monks. "Well, brother, you had something to ask me."

"Yes," said Veac. "Why are you here?"

"Does a man need a reason to attend a Church?"

"No, brother."

"But you are curious." Gartok nodded. "And I have no wish to insult those for whom I have a regard. A man in my trade never knows when he may need help. Doctors aren't always available but, on every world where there is war, monks are to be found."

Men with medical skill, with medicines and drugs to heal and to ease pain, with arts to end the torment of the dying. Neutral friends if nothing else and, always, they could be trusted.

And yet?

Gartok was a mercenary, shrewd, hard, selfish. And he had been almost the last man to see the old monk alive.

"You are kind, brother, but is there nothing else? Some personal regard, perhaps?"

Gartok shrugged. "You look for what isn't there, monk. I didn't know the old man. We spoke, exchanged a few words, a little news, and that is all. But another, years ago, as old, did me a service once. In fact he saved my life. Call my attendance here a belated tribute to that man." Turning he faced the doors behind which blazed the flame and, again, saluted. "Farewell, brother. May you find the peace you lived to teach." And then, oddly, added, "May we all find it."

The church never closed and, day or night, always someone was waiting to unburden themselves or to gain a little comfort. The sick too needed attention, mothers with babies covered in sores, older children with eyes thick with pus, themselves asking help and advice in order to avoid further pregnancies. Help and advice which was never refused.

It was dark by the time Veac had finished his duties, rising from a sick man to ease the ache in his back, looking down at the face now relaxed, the eyelids covering the eyes which flickered a little beneath the lids. One leg had been crushed, the wounds infected, suppurating, stinking with putrescence. The body burned with fever. A hospital could have taken care of the man, any competent doctor, but both would have asked for payment assured or in advance. The aid given by the monks was free.

"Brother!" Audin was a new arrival, young, fresh, eager to serve. "I am to relieve you. Do you have any special instructions as to the patients?"

"The man at the end of the first row is in extremis. He will most probably die before dawn. The woman in the second row is close to crisis so make sure that she is not alone for long. This man," he looked down at the figure, "is happy enough for the moment. I've given him subjective suggestion and will reenforce it later. Now we can do nothing but ease his pain and allow the drugs to do their work. Brother Biul?"

"Is waiting for you with Brother Thotan."

He was a big man, wide shoulders filling his robe, his head a naked ball, his hands holding the strength of a vice. A man who fought injustice and the ills of the universe as if they were personal enemies. The answer to all who considered the Church to be weak and helpless, those who thought monks to be cringing effeminates. Only his voice was soft and even then iron lurked beneath the gentle tones.

"I have completed my examination of your reports and findings and must admit there is no doubt as to the cause of Eldon's death. He was murdered. A poison was injected into his hand, probably by a sharpened fingernail or some instrument incorporating a hollow needle."

Veac said, boldly, "Wouldn't he have felt the pain?"

For a moment Thotan stared at the young monk, his eyes sunken in pits beneath his brows, the brown flecked with emerald, the white tinged with yellow.

"A good question, brother. Never be afraid to ask questions—how else can you find answers? Why didn't he feel pain when injected? Two reasons. One is that he simply didn't feel it. He could have been exposed to the cold for too long, his flesh numbed and unresponsive, or the instrument used could have been loaded with an anesthetic." His voice hardened as his finger stabbed at Veac. "The other?"

"He felt it but didn't comment. A jagged fingernail could have caused it or a broken button and, as you say, his hand must have been chilled." Hesitating Veac added, "The puncture was in the fleshy part of the palm. It is relatively insensitive to pain."

"And to anything else." Thotan nodded his satisfaction. "You have a sharp mind, brother, cultivate it. It could lead you far."

To a large church of his own, perhaps. To residence in a city where he would counsel the rich and influential. To Pace which held the second largest seminary of the Church, even to Hope which was the heart and fountainhead of the Universal Brotherhood. The world on which the High Monk was to be found, the records, the schools of training, the statues and adornments which generations of those who loved and worked for the objectives of the Church had built and donated.

Then he blinked, conscious of the sharp stare of the probing eyes. Could Thotan, as Biul had seemed to demonstrate, read minds? Telepathy was not unknown though those who held the talent paid for it in one way or another usually with physical malfunctions. Was the bulk all bone and muscle or the growth of wild cells? Was the head shaved or naturally bald.

Had the comment and praise, so casually uttered, been a test?

Veac straightened his shoulders. No monk could yield to fear and all had the right to be ambitious. It was only when that ambition became a thing of self rather than of aiding the unfortunate did it become a sin. And yet he had been close and could even have passed over the edge. The vision of Hope, the statues and items of price—avarice and pride of possession were both to be shunned. No monk could wear gems while others starved. No church could be built of gold while poverty reigned. Yet some things, while priceless, could not be sold.

"So we have an assassination," said Thotan. "Well, it isn't the first and I doubt if it will be the last, but monks are too scarce to be targets." He looked down at his massive hands. They were clenched—at times it was hard to be forgiving. "The question is—who wanted Eldon dead and why? We know how he was killed; the derelict who asked for help when he returned from the field. The man must have been waiting, primed, placed like a weapon ready to fire. Dead, of course?"

"He was dying when he arrived," said Biul. "He was washed and fed and given drugs to ensure rest and sleep. He never woke. Only after Eldon had been found did we investigate. It seems a natural death but, though old, he was strong and I grew suspicious. Tests showed the presence of poison. More from where it came. The rest you know."

The report which had been sent over the hybeam and which had brought him from a nearby world to make what investigation he could. As yet he had discovered nothing new.

"Gartok," he said. "He was cleared at the official inquiry, I know, but that was a casual affair. Anything more?" He pursed his lips as Veac told him about the man's attendance at the cremation, his salute. "Mercenaries are superstitious and he could have told you the truth. And what connection could there be between him and Eldon? Yet a man isn't killed without reason. If possible we must find it."

As a protection. As a warning to others who might be tempted to attack the monks and the Church which they served. And as a comfort to those same monks who would be bolstered by the assurance that to be humble was not to be weak.

Things Veac thought about as, later, he searched through Eldon's possessions. They were few—a monk owned only what he could carry, but each held some strong memory and each had helped to soften the harshness of the chamber in which he lived and slept. Light splintered from glass embedded in a polished scrap of wood, the edge of the mineral flecked so as to create a razor-sharp edge. Perhaps it had served as a razor or even as a scalpel. A scrap of fabric bore an elaborate design of knots. A piece of stone had been rubbed into a smooth complexity of curves and concavities over which the fingers travelled in sensuous caress; a worry-stone striped with rippled rainbows. A painting done in oils of a young man with a fresh, open face. Eldon himself? Veac doubted it, few monks wanted to be reminded of their past and the portrait was probably that of a relative or an old associate. Putting it down he looked about the chamber. There had been something else, he remembered, a book in which the old man had written from time to time. A record of his achievements, he had once explained. A slim journal containing fifty years of his life.

Veac couldn't find it. Searching he found a battered medical handbook, another containing a list of useful herbs together with illustrations and instructions as to preparation, a third which held a collection of poems. But the journal was not to be found.

Going to the door he opened it. Thotan had arrived accompanied by Audin and another. He waited outside for the room to be cleared, a small, slim man with liquid eyes and a skin like oiled chocolate.

"Brother Anz, a moment if you please." Veac stepped back into the chamber. When the other joined him he said, "Have you seen anyone enter or leave this room today? Anyone at all?"

"Yourself and, earlier, Brother Thotan."

"Anyone else?"

"A woman. She came to clean, I think, at least she carried a bucket and held a broom. But I only saw her as she walked along the corridor."

"Describe her," Veac nodded as the man obeyed. The woman was, as the monk had suspected, a cleaner—one of many volunteers probably on her way to the infirmary or kitchen and taking a short-cut through the living quarters. He would speak to her later and advise against her continuing the habit. "Thank you brother."

The book must have been lost somehow but, as Veac was turning toward the door, Anz said, "A moment, brother. I remember now. Before I saw the woman and before I had entered the passage a man passed me coming from this direction. I suppose he could have entered this room if he had wished but why he should eludes me. Perhaps he wanted an interview with yourself or Brother Biul. He was big with a scarred face and—"

"A moment!" Veac described Kars Gartok. "Yes?"

"It is possible. I only caught a glimpse but that could be the man."

The mercenary a thief? His breed were all thieves even if they called their loot the spoils of war but would such a man steal a book? And of what possible use could the private journal of a dead monk be to such a man?

The auctioneer's hammer fell with a thud.

"Fifty men, semi-trained, sold to Ophren Hyde! The next lot consists of three trained weapon-guidance engineers. All fully experienced having fought with Arkill's Avengers and the Poloshenic Corps. I start with five thousand . . . five . . . five . . ."

A man called, "Their contract?"

"Open to negotiation. Purchase price refunded if transfer arranged. One tour of duty mandatory. Do you bid six?"

"Six."

They would go for nine and the buyer would be either Kuang Tao or Brod Lacour. Only they owned the equipment which would make such a price worth the outlay. And, if either bought, then something must be moving which as yet he was still ignorant.

Damn Othurine and her tears!

Charl Embris shifted irritably in his seat as another parcel was offered for sale. This time it was a score of battle-hardened mercenaries, good men and reliable and far better than the cheaper semi-trained and basic material which usually was to be found on the block. But times were hard and even good men were willing to sign up for bed and board and a few basic comforts which certain women, also on contract, were willing to supply.

"Three," droned the auctioneer. "No? Gentlemen you amaze me. "Two then, let us try two. Still you hesitate? Then let us forget the reserve. Name your own figure. What am I bid for a score of experienced fighters?"

Embris touched the button of the instrument in his pocket. Far to one side a man said, "Five hundred!"

"Five—surely you jest!" The auctioneer, an old man, had his pride. "I will start with one thousand. If there are no bids the lot will be withdrawn. The reputation of Ilyard must be maintained. These are trained and skilled soldiers, gentlemen! Do I have to remind you of that? Now, who will open the bidding?"

"One thousand."

"Thank you. I will accept bids in hundreds."

Again Embris thumbed the button and, like a marionette triggered by the radioed impulse, his agent lifted his hand.

"Eleven."

Another man, "Twelve!"

"Thirteen!"

"Fifteen!"

That would be Gin Peng always impatient or intent on forcing up the price so as to weaken later competition. His bid was secret, of course, as was any dealer's of note. Even a good reputation would inflate the price and, if known factions were opposed, then the fur really flew.

"Fifteen? Any advance on fifteen?" The auctioneer poised his hammer. "Going . . . going . . . gone!"

Well, if Peng had made the bid, then good luck to him. There would be other lots and more men and it would do no harm to conserve wealth and outlay until he had a market for anything he might decide to buy. A conservative outlook and one which would hardly make a man a fortune but he could afford to coast for a little. Forever if it came to that—he had money enough to retire. But how else could he occupy his time? What could ever replace the thrill of buying and selling men, of manipulating supplies, of weighing the scales against an opponent and arranging private alliances, deals, surrenders?

"My lord!" His aide was deferential, his voice low as he stooped over the back of the chair. "There is a man requesting an audience. A mercenary. Kars Gartok—I have his record."

It was a good one, at least the man knew his trade and wouldn't waste his time as so many others did or tried to do. Embris looked up and around, seeing nothing of interest either on or near the block, noting too that several seats were empty. He would lose nothing by leaving and could gain much.

"Give me an hour. Have the man wait in the iron-room of my house. See that he is fed. A meal will take up most of the time."

And the wine which went with it helped to ease his tongue. Kars Gartok recognized the danger and sipped sparingly at the rich and potent liquid an attendant kept pouring into his glass. The food was another matter and he ate well, chewing at succulent meats and spiced vegetables, dabbing at the juice which ran from his mouth and over his chin.

Once he saw the look of disdain the attendant threw at him and smiled behind the napkin. Let the fool sneer—the food he ate now would see him through days if necessary. And the report the man would make would serve its purpose later.

A game, he thought, as the dishes were cleared and only the wine left standing before him. In life everything was a game. A man gambled for riches, for comfort, for ease and, if he had to set his life on the board to win them, well, that was the nature of the play. Win all or lose all— a fair wager. Only the weak were afraid to take the chance, clinging to a life little better than a hell in order simply to survive. Fools who overvalued the few years of existence they could expect. What difference if life ended now or in a score of years? Ten? One? Against the immensity of time what a small thing a year was.

"You dream," said Embris as he entered the room. "Of past victories, perhaps?"

"Of future gain, my lord." Rising Gartok bowed—those with titles liked them to be used and it cost nothing to be polite. "And I was admiring the room."

A lie, decorative metal meant nothing to him, not even when it was fashioned into edged and pointed weapons gracing the black leather beneath in a host of chilling glitters.

"A notion of my son's. He—" Embris broke off, shaking his head. "Never mind that. You have something to say to me?"

"A matter of mutual interest, my lord, and perhaps one of common profit." Gartok helped himself to the wine. "I saw you and your lady in the church. The death of the monk obviously had affected you both. I too had attended to pay my respects—did you know that I was almost the last to see him alive?"

"I did not." Embris looked at the decanter. "You appreciate the wine?"

"And your generosity in offering it, my lord." Gartok lifted his goblet and drank. "And now to business. As you might expect a man such as myself often picks up items of information which could be converted into profitable enterprises. Your trade is in the supplying of men and arms—mine is using them. We have a common interest. So, if I hint that there is a world ripe for a little war, that there are those interested in seeing it takes place—well?"

"Continue."

"At the moment it is an aborted conflict. Apparently the instigator died. But what was once planned need not be ignored. Naturally an investigation needs to be made and so we come to the purpose of my visit." Gartok set down his goblet. "To be plain—would you be interested in backing me? In return you get the sole concession of the loot of a world."

Embris said, flatly, "I have been made such promises before."

"Am I making promises?" Gartok shook his head, smiling. "I am stating probable facts. I have your confidence? Then let me mention a name. Gydapen Prabang. It strikes a chord?" His eyes were hard, direct, gimlets

searching the other's face. "Gydapen Prabang," he said
again. "He bought some guns which were shipped via Harald. Perhaps they originated on Ilyard. You could even
have handled the deal."

"And if I did?"

"Then surely all is plain. If not then others might be interested. Kuang Tao, perhaps, or Gin Peng? Both are always eager to make a small investment in the hope of vast
returns." Taking up his goblet Gartok sipped at his wine.
Then, casually, he said, "This room was decorated by your
son, you say?"

"It was his idea."

"He must spend many happy hours here." Gartok
blinked as if realizing he could have made a mistake. "I
take it that he is well?"

"He is—away just now."

"Children." Gartok shrugged. "At times I thank God I
have no need to acknowledge any I may have sired. A
man has enough worry without adding to his burden. A
wife, children—what need has a mercenary for such
things? A fine son like yours leaves an aching void when
he is absent. How would you feel if he should die? To love
is to store grief for the future. None is immortal."

"Tomir's a fine young man."

"I know. I know. I've heard of him. Ambitious too so I
understand. An eagle eager to spread his wings. With your
help he could command his own corps and he wouldn't
want for men to serve under his orders. A pity he isn't
here. If he was we could have done business together."

"Your business is with me."

"Perhaps. You don't seem to be interested." Gartok was
indifferent. "But it's worth investigating, don't you think?
And quickly if at all. Others could be interested and might
already be acting. A wise man would make certain he
wasn't left out in the cold. An entire world—the dream of
every mercenary. A whole planet waiting to be exploited—and you hesitate to spend a little to make it
yours."

Embris said, harshly, "I have men of my own should I
need such work done."

"True—and those men are known. How long would it
take before a half-dozen others knew exactly what you in-

tended? A world on the edge of war, nobles enraged, an offer made, troops employed and what should have been a minor operation engrossed with a change of power turns into a full-scale conflict. Who will be safe then? How to reap the rewards?" Gartok shrugged and drank the rest of his wine. "It seems I'm wasting my time."

"Maybe not. Where is this world you speak of?"

"Somewhere."

"Its name?"

Gartok smiled and lifted the decanter. "Shall we discuss terms?"

Chapter FIVE

Lavinia said, "Earl, this is a waste of time. We should be training men and getting ready to fight. To hold our own. Instead all you've done for days now is to take photographs. There will be time for sightseeing when we are safe."

She sat at the controls of the raft, half-turned so as to display her profile, the swell of breasts and the glinting mane of her hair. The bar of silver which broke the raven cascade was a slash of reflected brilliance.

A beautiful woman and a clever one in her fashion. Dumarest studied the lines and contours of the face, the eyes, deep-set beneath strong brows, the lips full, the lower pouted in betraying sensuality. The cheekbones were high, the jaw strong, the nose patrician. His eyes fell lower. Were the mounds of her breasts swollen? Was the waist a little thicker than it had been? The curve of her belly more prominent?

Was she really pregnant or had she lied?

"Earl?" She was impatient, wanting arguments or explanations or perhaps only his attention. For long hours she had done nothing but send the raft on a carefully plotted path at a carefully maintained height. Work for a machine but they had none sophisticated enough and Dumarest had not wanted to use anyone else. "How much longer must we do this?"

"This is the last leg."

"You've seen all you want?" Her tone was bitter. "Is this land worth holding? My ancestors thought so—some of them died for it."

"And more have sweated for it," he said, dryly. "And gained just enough to hold their bodies when they died."

"Serfs," she said. "Retainers."

"People."

He turned as the instrument mounted at the back of the vehicle gave a sharp, brittle sound. An automatic camera set on struts so as to allow the lens a clear field of view, a timing mechanism taking one frame after another at regular intervals. The signal had been to warn him the magazine was close to exhaustion.

"Be ready to halt, Lavinia." He watched the counter, heard again the warning. "Now!"

Dumarest changed the magazine as the raft ceased its forward progress then leaned over the side of the open-bodied craft to study the ground below. It was rough, the surface torn and savage, bare of vegetation aside from patches of scrub. Yellow rock and sand edged the rims of crevasses, the dim bulk of massive boulders showing at their bottoms, streaks of mineral brightness lying like a tracery of filagree in the murky shadows.

A harsh place but beneath it could lie thick veins of minerals; rare metals, gems, valuable chemicals, fossil fuels, all things for which more sophisticated worlds would pay high prices to obtain. Refineries could be built and mines started. Men could be hired together with skilled technicians. The old ways would vanish as the retainers now bound to the great Families found economic independence. New towns would be built, new fields established. Traffic would fill the air, the deserts would bloom and ships would come streaming in from space with their holds stuffed with luxuries and essentials in exchange for the wealth torn from the bowels of this backward planet.

It had happened before. He had seen it happen—but it wouldn't happen here. Not while the Sungari ruled over what lay beneath the surface and the Pact had to be maintained.

"Earl!" Lavinia looked at him from where she sat. "Earl, I'm sorry. Can you forgive a stupid woman?"

"No—not when she isn't really stupid but just chooses to act that way."

"One day I'll get used to you," she said, softly. "I don't know when that day will be, maybe not for years, but it will come. When it does I'll understand why you do what you do. This raft, these photographs, why are they so necessary?"

"You said we should fight, remember?"

"With men and guns and courage."

"There are more ways than one to fight," he said, flatly. "And the least efficient is to set one man against another. It's also the most expensive both in terms of money and human misery. You claim to love this land—do you want to see it destroyed?"

"Of course not!"

"What do you think would happen if armies met and heavy weapons were used? The castle is strong, but a single missile could reduce it to rubble. Your retainers might be brave, but what good is bravery when flesh and hair and bone are burning beneath chemical heat? In such a war there are no victors. Only the mercenaries stand to gain from loot and pay and even then too many of them will die."

"Scum!"

"Workers," he corrected. "Men willing to do a dirty job. They don't demand that you hire them."

"Beasts! Predators!"

"If you hire men to kill you don't expect them to act like a crowd of monks." Dumarest checked the camera, "Turn, move to the right for three hundred yards, head south and maintain course."

"Due south?"

"No. Run a course parallel to the other. Speed and height the same."

He sat as she obeyed, leaning over the edge of the raft and watching as the ground streamed past below. Not all of Zakym was desert, much of it was fertile soil bearing a variety of crops; good, well-watered dirt which was the source of the majority of food. Other areas were less fertile but supported enough vegetation to provide grazing for beasts. There was a little mining in certain areas. A little fishing on the coast far to the west. A little industry—everything on the world was little. A bad place for any traveller to be stranded. In more ways than one he had been lucky.

"Earl!"

Dumarest hadn't needed the warning. He had seen the mote which came directly toward them; a raft, larger than their own and bearing pennants striped in gold and orange. In it, attended by a half-dozen men, Jait Elz, the young son of Alcorus, glared his annoyance.

"What right have you to traverse these lands?" His tone was peevish despite his efforts to make it strong and commanding. A boy, barely a man, as yet unsuited for the exercise of authority. "Have you permission?"

Lavinia said sharply, "Don't be a fool, Jait. Since when have I needed permission to cross this terrain?"

"You should have asked."

"Asked who? Alcorus? Who?" Her sneer was plain. "Your father has more sense. Perhaps, when next you want to fly your produce over the estates of Belamosk, you will gain as much. Certainly you will remember this stupidity. Your lands are bound by mine and those of Prabang."

"We have no quarrel with you."

"I see." She glanced at Dumarest. "You have no liking for the Lord Dumarest, is that it? Have you forgotten that he is a ruler of this world? That his estates are as large as those held by your Family?"

"They—"

"Are his!" she snapped. "Voted to him by the Council together with the title. You talk to the Lord Dumarest Prabang when you address him and it would be wise of you not to forget it." Her voice lowered, became a feral purr, "Or do you wish to challenge him? If so I am sure he will be pleased to accommodate you. It could be settled here before your friends. Or did you want to goad him into challenging you?"

"No!" Jait had paled. "No!"

"Then—?"

"I came to intercept you. To bring you a message." Sweat beaded the young man's face. "The Council—"

"I know about the Council. Is there anything else?

As the rafts parted and the larger dwindled she said, bitterly. "You know what all that was about, Earl?"

"It's obvious. They're closing in."

"Like animals eager for prey." The raft jerked a little under her hands. "Even that young fool thought he could bait you. How many others will have the same idea?" And then, quietly, as if speaking to herself, "How many of them will you have to kill before we are safe?"

Suchong had the chair. He slammed down the gavel and as the noise died, said, "I pronounce this meeting of the Council of Zakym open. A quorum is present. What we decide will be binding as has been mutually agreed. The first item for discussion is—"

A man rose, interrupting the chairman. He said, formally. "A question. Is this a public meeting?"

"No. Of course not."

"Then I protest at the presence of a stranger." The man glanced at Dumarest where he sat at Lavinia's side. "One among us had no right to be here."

"Nonsense!" Lavinia rose to her feet. "You are talking about the new owner of Prabang, right? This Council voted him the lands and the title. At the time they had cause to be grateful."

The protester ignored the sarcasm. "But not the seat. I was absent at the time but I have read the minutes. No mention was made of him taking Gydapen's place on the Council. He was not put up and accepted. If I have misinterpreted the intention then I apologize but the record is plain."

"The bastard!" Lavinia sucked in her breath with a vicious hissing. "Earl—"

"Leave it!" His voice was low but sharp. "Don't argue about it. This has been arranged. If you protest too strongly they could expel you for this session on the grounds of undue interest. Stay and do what you can but ride with the majority."

"Agree with them?"

"Lie to them. Smile and be gracious and delay things if you can. If you can't make friends at least avoid making enemies."

Good advice if not easy to follow. She followed him with her eyes as Dumarest rose, bowed to the chair and left the room. With his leaving the place seemed suddenly colder, the carved heads adorning the fresco beneath the ceiling adopting a more hostile expression. A trick of fancy, she knew, wood could not change expression, but flesh and blood could and it was no fancy that, as Dumarest left, men settled and relaxed and yielded to a minor triumph.

Alcorus for one and it proved again the brittleness of

friendship. Had his son been sent to test the opposition or had the boy, listening to the words spoken by his father, felt safe in anticipating what was to come. Roland? He surely would remain loyal for her sake if for nothing else, but he too held a certain satisfaction. Dumarest could have told her why, but as yet she was ignorant of the true extent of his jealousy. Suchong was, she thought, neutral even though he backed the new heir. Navalok the same. Taiyuah, unexpectedly present, sat fumbling a carved box inset with a fine mesh. A container for one of his precious worms, perhaps, or a coccoon. To him the insects were more important than humans.

Again Suchong slammed his gavel on the table.

"Let us come to order if you please. Has anyone any further objection to the formation of this Council? No? Then I move that we decide the status of Earl Dumarest, the present Lord of Prabang. Do we admit him to the Council?"

"Yes," said Lavinia. "He has earned the right."

"Then let us vote on the matter. Those in favor?"

"A moment!" Alcorus lifted a hand. "I am not arguing as to his right to be put up and will abide by the vote no matter which way it falls, but is there any need of such a vote at all? We have discussed with him the desirability of Gydapen's son taking over the estate and he has agreed to sell. As he will not be with us long what purpose can be served by taking him among us?"

"The giving of honor and the recognition of his services." Taiyuah looked up from his box. "Are we so small-minded that we begrudge him that?"

"Thank you, Khatya." Lavinia looked at the circle of faces. "At least one among you has the courage to admit what we owe to Earl. And he has agreed to accommodate you in your plan so why the hostility? Incidentally, has the land yet been assessed as to value?"

Roland cleared his throat. "Not exactly," he admitted. "There are complications as I suspected there would be. How to gain a true figure? As yet the estimates vary between one sum and another eight times as much."

"Strike a medium," said Navalok. "Give him a quarter of the average. He agreed to a quarter."

"True, but—" Roland broke off, shaking his head.

"Even a quarter of the average would be more than we could easily find."

The reason for their hostility and Jait's stupid accosting of the raft. Men out of their depth and unsure of which way to turn. To them the world of finance was a mystery, business a closed book. Farmers, breeders, dealing in inter-family barter, buying what they needed with the profits of goods—money they never saw. And, if Gydapen's son was growing impatient?

Lavinia said, loudly, "If it comes down to a question of money then why can't the proposed new heir meet the bill? After all it is he who stands to gain the most. Surely he doesn't expect us to buy his land for him?"

"We gave it away," snapped Alcorus. "It is up to us to regain it."

Or tell the heir to go to hell, but Lavinia didn't suggest that, remembering Dumarest's advice. *If you can't make friends at least don't make enemies.*

But, at times, it was hard.

There were no beggars on Zakym. The streets of the town were clean, the houses neat, the people dressed in decent clothing adorned with the symbols of their Families. Things Dumarest had noticed before and noted again as he stepped from the Council Building and across the open space which occupied the center of the town. He had seen similar conditions on other worlds but here were no armed and watchful guards to maintain the facade, no stinking mass of hovels into which the poor were confined, no Lowtown to hold the stranded and desperate.

A nice, clean, easy-going world in which a man could manage to survive if he was willing to fit in. One which resisted the exploiters and the things they would bring; the whores and touts and fighters and gamblers. The vice and degradation. The crime. The pain. The human parasites who would put the most blood-hungry of their natural counterparts to shame.

A good world, but the field was empty of ships and the trading post seemed deserted. Dumarest halted within the doorway, smelling the combined scents of spices and leather, of oil, perfumes, fabrics, dried herbs, pounded meats—a blend of odors which always clung to such places and gave each a haunting familiarity.

"Earl!" In the shadows something stirred, took the shape of a man, came forward with a flash of white teeth in the ebon of a caste-marked face. "I wondered how long it would be before you came in."

"Jmombota!" Dumarest lifted a hand in greeting. "Anything new?"

"On Zakym?" The agent shrugged. "During the last period of delusia I saw my grandmother who told me that I was wasting my time here. A waste, don't you think? I hardly needed a visit from the dead to tell me that. As I hardly need you to tell me this world has compensations."

"Was I going to tell you that?"

"People do. All the time. But never, when I offer to allow them to take my place, do they show the slightest eagerness to take advantage of my generosity." The agent glanced at an ornate clock. "A drink?"

Dumarest said, ironically, "Have we the time?"

"I was checking. The suns are well apart now and we have hours before they close. Before delusia I'm going to take something to put me well asleep and to keep me in that state. I was never fond of my grandmother even when she was alive and now that she's dead I can't stand the sight of her." He laughed and produced a bottle. "To your health!"

"To yours!"

They drank and stood for a while in companionable silence. They had little in common either in race or creed but both were men, both alien to the culture of this world, and both knew the meaning of loneliness.

As he poured fresh drinks the agent said, "The ships will arrive when they come, Earl."

"Can you read my mind?"

"Do I have to? Each time you come into town you look at the field. I've seen your eyes and recognize what they hold. I've seen it in other men and, once I think, I had it myself. Once, but no longer—a wife and child took care of that. They provide strong anchors for a man with a tendency to roam."

Dumarest made no comment.

"Sweet traps, someone once called them," continued the

agent. "Soft hands which cling and can never be shaken loose." And then, casually, he added, "I understand that you are selling your lands."

"So?"

"I wondered why. Things hard-won should not be thrown away. And it is hard to estimate a fair price. You could be cheated, my friend."

"Or dead."

"That too, but we grow solemn." The agent smiled and lifted his glass in a question. The smile widened as Dumarest shook his head. "A wise man once said that happiness can never be found in a bottle, only truth. And truth, when found, can be painful."

"You know a lot of wise men," said Dumarest. "And have a lot of friends. Is Mbom Chelhar one of them?"

"No."

"But you know him?"

"As I know you, Earl. Less well and with less pleasure. He is away at the moment, a guest of someone, I think. Probably examining a herd of some kind. He is an agent for the purchase of beasts so I understand. You see? My knowledge is vague."

Dumarest doubted it. "Is he expected back soon?"

"Perhaps."

"When you see him give him a message. Or get one to him. He is invited to dine at the Castle Delamosk tonight." He added, blandly, "A matter of business. Can the man be trusted?"

For answer the agent picked up a dried fruit from an open container. "Look at this, Earl. When growing in its natural state it is a thing of beauty, apparently succulent and offering the promise of pleasant nourishment. But the show is a lie. Bite into it and you would find the taste of gall and the attributes of medication. A wise man does not trust what he sees."

A warning—and a Hausi did not lie. As he threw the fruit back into its box Dumarest said, "A most useful piece of information. And one which should be rewarded. It is obvious that the Lady Lavinia will need a shrewd agent to handle any business transaction which may arise from the selling of her beasts. It would be to her interest to deal through you and, naturally the usual commissions will be paid. That is if you are willing to accept the commission?"

A good arrangement and one offering mutual advantage. Smiling the agent reached for the bottle.

"I shall be happy to serve. With contacts like yourself, Earl, I may yet achieve my ambition to retire to a palace on Hitew. A small one, naturally, but large enough for the garden to be filled with the singing blooms of Zlethe. There I shall sit as the sun descends and merge with the music which the plants and I shall create. Who knows? I may even become a famous composer. You will join me in a toast to that?" His tone changed a little, became more meaningful. "Let us drink to the ambitions of us both, my friend. May we each achieve our heart's desire!"

Again they stood in silence each engrossed in his own private dream, then the agent, setting down his glass said, "An interesting item of news, Earl. A wrecked vessel was discovered drifting in the Rift. A small trader by the shape. Incredibly it still contained a living man. They took him to Fralde."

Chapter SIX

The building was of stone, massive blocks fused together with the heat of lasers, windows shaped in tall, pointed arches, the stories rearing one above the other against a somber sky. Leaden stone set in leaden grounds against leaden clouds. On Fralde everything was grey.

Director Ningsia matched his environment. A short, blocky man with skin bearing creases as if it too were made of stone. Grey hair swept back from a high forehead. His mouth was thin, the lips bloodless, the eyes slanted ovoids beneath up-rising brows. His uniform was grey; only the insignia of his rank riding high on his left bicep shone with luminous emerald.

A neatly precise man dedicated to the stern dictates of his culture. One who believed in the submergence of self to the good of the whole.

He said, "Cyber Ardoch the matter is being dealt with in the usual way. The man is beyond any aid we can give."

"But he is still alive?"

"Amazingly, yes. His continued existence is a contravention of all accepted standards of the survival-attributes of the human race. My own speculation is that he has certain mutant traits which has increased his defense mechanisms to an incredible extent. The condition of his epidermis and the internal decay alone would have killed any normal man. An interesting specimen which is, of course, the reason we have devoted so much time and material to his welfare."

An attitude the cyber could appreciate.

"You have information as to the original situation?"

"Of course. The rescue vessel was a small ship operating from this planet and engaged in plotting the energy-flows occuring in this region of the Rift. Its detectors spotted mass and an investigation was made. The wreck was little more than twisted metal as was to be expected but, incredibly, a portion of it remained intact. Apparently the sole occupant had sealed himself within and insulated the compartment with a pattern of meshed wires fed by battery-power. In effect he had, somehow, managed to heterodyne the destructive energies of the Rift. Naturally he had also a supply of food and water which, together with quick-time—but surely you have read the report?"

"I have."

"There is nothing more I can add." Ningsia made a small gesture, one of dismissal. "A full autopsy will be made after the man has died and the report completed. If you are interested I will see to it that a copy is sent to you."

Ardoch said, evenly, "That is not why I am here, Director. It is essential that I see the man."

"See him?" Ningsia frowned. "What purpose would that serve the patient? He is comatose."

"Even so, Director, I must insist."

The cyber didn't raise his voice, it continued to be the trained, even modulation carefully designed to eliminate all irritant factors, but the Director was under no illusion. The Cyclan was powerful and the cyber was a servant of the Cyclan.

As he hesitated the cyber continued, "It is a small matter. surely? It will not inconvenience the running of your hospital. All I require is access to the patient and the services of a medical practitioner who will obey my orders. That and privacy."

Privacy? Ningsia's frown deepened—what business could the cyber have with the near-dead survivor of a wrecked vessel? Yet how could he refuse to cooperate? Fralde was on the verge of completing negotiations with a sister world—an alliance which held great promise. The Cyclan had been of tremendous help in gaining maximum advantage. To deny the request would be to risk his own advancement and to court punishment for his lack of discernment.

Stiffly he snapped to attention. "I am at your full disposal, Cyber Ardoch. The patient is in ward 87, bed 152.

Doctor Wuhu will attend you." He added, bleakly, "He will do everything you ask."

Wuhu was a younger edition of the Director; a little less stiff, a little less tall. Following him through the hospital the cyber, by contrast, was a pillar of flame. His scarlet robe with the great seal of the Cyclan glowing on its breast reflected the light in a host of ruby shimmers. His shaven skull, rising above the thrown-back cowl, looked emaciated but was simply bone and muscle devoid of fat. As was the rest of his hard, lean body.

To a cyber food was something to fuel the metabolism and nothing else. Fat was a waste of both food and energy, unwanted tissue which slowed mental processes and physical function. Like emotion it was unessential to the working of the intellect.

And no cyber could feel emotion.

An operation performed at puberty on the thalamus reenforced earlier training and divorced the mind from the impulses of the body. Ardoch could feel no hate, no fear, no anger, no love. A flesh and blood robot he followed the doctor through the bleak corridors of the hospital, indifferent to the cries, the moans, the sounds of anguish coming from the beds ranked in the vast wards.

Indifferent also to the glimpses of doctors working in operating theatres, the machines, the attendants, the creatures on which they worked. People were basically machines; those who healed them were engineers repairing the biological fabrications. They were merciful in their fashion—but efficiency came first.

An attitude of which the cyber approved.

"In here," said Wuhu as they approached a door. "Far down on the left."

"You have mobile screens?"

"Of course."

"See they are placed in readiness. I understand the patient is comatose—have drugs on hand together with a hypogun. You use such a device?"

"We are not primitives," said the young man, stiffly. "May I ask what drugs you intend to use?" He blinked at the answer, his momentary hope of scoring a small victory over the other's ignorance vanishing as he realized the cyber knew as much about medicine as himself. Even so he uttered a warning. "They are potent compounds. Excessive use or certain combinations could result in convulsions and death."

Ardoch said, "Your orders were plain, were they not?"

"To obey you—yes, they were plain."

"Then do as you were directed. See to the screens, obtain the drugs and equipment but, first, show me the patient."

He lay on a narrow cot, a mass of decaying tissue, the face distorted, the cheeks sunken, the lids closed over the twitching eyes. Beneath the thin sheet, which was his only cover, the body seemed distorted, one leg ending in a stump, the hips swollen, asymmetrical. The skin was scaled, cracked and oozing a thin, odorous pus. A crust had formed at the edges of the mouth.

He was not alone.

Ardoch stiffened at the sight of the cowled figure which sat beside the cot, hands resting on the patient's arm, his voice a low, soothing murmur as he enhanced the hypnotic trance into which he had thrown the sick man.

"You are standing on a meadow bright with little flowers with a brook running along one end and trees giving shade at the other. There are friends with you, a girl whom you love and who loves you in return. Soon you are to be married but now you are young and filled with the joy of life. The sun is warm and together you will swim in the clear water. You can feel it now. You are touching it and your friends are laughing and your girl is smiling and you are content. From the trees come . . ."

The monk paid no attention as the cyber halted at his side, concentrating on the hypnotic suggestions he was implanting in the mind of the dying man so that, at least, he would know a brief if final happiness.

As Wuhu came to join him Ardoch said, "Does this man have permission to do what he is doing?"

"Brother Verin is known to the hospital. He comes and goes as he pleases."

"That is not what I asked."

"Yes, he has permission to tend the patients. When we have done all that we can do then he seems able to give added comfort. It costs nothing."

"I understand the patient was comatose."

"He was, brother." Verin rose to his feet to stand beside the cyber, his brown robe in sharp contrast to the scarlet, the homespun to the shimmering weave. "But there are ways to bring comfort even to a mind locked in on itself."

"You have used drugs?"

The monk shrugged aside the accusation. "I have used nothing but touch and words, brother. They are all that is needed for anyone wise in their application. Words and—" he let irony edge his tone "—a little understanding. Men are not machines no matter what those who would find it convenient for them to be may claim."

Watching them Wuhu sensed the mutual antagonism which wreathed them like an invisible cloud. Masked yet it was there as they faced each other. Like natural enemies, a cat and dog perhaps, or the opposing articles of differing faiths. The monk who believed in love and tolerance and the cyber who believed in nothing but the cold logic of emotionless reason which had no room for sentiment and no place for mercy. The Church and the Cyclan face to face over the dying.

If it came to a war between them who would win?

An academic question as the young doctor was quick to realize. Those who had dedicated their lives to the doctrine of peace would never seek to kill and those who followed reason would never yield to the final stupidity. Between them would be no bloody battles or corrosive wars in which planets would burn and men wither like flies in winter. And yet, even so, always between them there would be conflict.

But, if by some incredible twist of fate actual war should rise between them, Wuhu would back the Cyclan. They were not afraid to exterminate.

And yet who could assess the stubborn resolve of a crusade?

He shook his head, aware that such speculation had no place here at this time, if ever, and the moment of strain passed as Ardoch turned toward him.

"Where are the screens?"

They arrived as the monk, after a final glance at the dying man, moved quietly down the ward to where another patient was in need of his ministration. He and all the occupants of the neatly set rows of beds, vanished from sight as attendants set the screens into place and turned the area around the bed into an oasis of privacy.

"The drugs." Ardoch gestured at the physician. "This man is in a deep, hypnotic trance. I want him brought out of it and his mind placed in a state of conscious awareness. It would be as well if you recognized the urgency of the situation."

In other words kill him if it was necessary but wake him long enough to listen and answer. Wuhu was aware of the implication but, a physician of Fralde, he had no compunction at cutting short a life which was already lost. And it would be an act of mercy to shorten the dying man's anguish.

As he stepped forward to lift the charged hypogun and rest it against the flaccid throat of the patient the cyber caught his arm.

"A moment. I wish to check the medication." He twisted a knob and ejected the charge. "As I suspected. You were about to give far too high a dose of pain-killer. Coupled with the rest it would have given him a momentary euphoria. You forget that he is experiencing subjective pleasure. Before he can be of use that must be eradicated. Here." He handed back the instrument. "I want him awake, aware and in pain. Commence!"

Silently the doctor obeyed. The hiss of the air-blast carrying the drugs into the patient's bloodstream was followed, within seconds, by a groan.

It yielded to a scream.

"God! God the pain! The pain!"

The voice was thick, slobbering, the words almost lost in the liquid gurgle of phlegm, the dissolving tissue of decaying lungs. On the cover the hands clenched, fingers digging into the fabric, pus thick at cracked joints.

"The pain!"

"It will be eased if you cooperate." Ardoch sat on the edge of the bed and leaned towards the contorted face. Reflected light from his robe gave the pasty flesh an unreal flush of artificial health. "Your name? Your name, man! Your name!"

"Fatshan. Fatshan of the *Sleethan.* The engineer. We

got caught in the Rift. A generator—for God's sake do something about the pain."

The hypogun hissed as the cyber gestured. Wuhu stepped back, eyes and ears alert, Ningsia, for one, would be grateful for any information he could gain and convey. As if guessing his thoughts Ardoch held out his hand.

"Give me the hypogun and go."

"Leave my patient?"

"To me, yes. And I shall not remind you again of your instructions." As the man left the cyber stared at the dying engineer. "Look at me," he commanded. "At the robe I wear. You have seen others like it before I think. On Harald? On board the *Sleethan*?"

The only pleasure a cyber could experience was the glow of mental achievement and, as the dying man nodded, Ardoch knew it to the full. A prediction confirmed and his skill demonstrated without question. From a handful of facts, diverse data collected, correlated, woven into a pattern he had extrapolated the logical sequence of events. An attribute possessed by all cybers, the fruit of long and arduous training which enhanced natural talent, the thing which made them both desired and disliked by those who paid for their services.

Would a certain pattern gain favor in the markets? A manufacturer of clothing could find the answer—at a price, the predictions as to sales and shifts in fashion guiding him and ensuring the maximum protection against loss, the maximum anticipation of profit.

Should a proposed marriage be cancelled or the original intention pursued? A cyber would point out the path such a union would take as appertaining to the shift and balance of power, the influence of possible children, the merging of interests, the alienation of potential enemies.

To hire the services of the Cyclan was to ensure success and to minimize error. Once used the temptation to take advantage of such advice could not be resisted. So the Cyclan grew in power and influence, with cybers at every court, in every sphere of influence, predicting the sequence of events following any action, weaving a scarlet-tinted web.

Sitting, listening to the liquid gurgle of Fatshan's voice,

Ardoch filled in the parts left unsaid, verifying pervious knowledge, endorsing made predictions.

"On Harald men took passage on board the *Sleethan*," he said. "Cyber Broge, his acolyte and a man called Dumarest. Verify!"

The ruined face lolled on the pillow. "Gone! All gone!"

"Dead?" A doubt to be resolved and a search to be ended. "Did they die in the ship with the others?" He leaned forward as the bloated head signaled a negative. "They did not die."

"Not in the Rift. They vanished before we reached Zakym."

"Vanished?"

"Disappeared." The engineer reared. "The pain? I can't stand the pain! For God's sake give me something for it."

"You'll talk? Cooperate?" The hypogun hissed as the man grunted agreement, the instrument delivering its reward of mercy. A double dose; the drugs which numbed pain were accompanied by others which gave a false confidence. "Tell me!"

"We were on Harald," wheezed the engineer. "But you know that. The cyber and his acolyte took Dumarest prisoner. The captain had no choice but to agree. The reward—you understand."

A free-trader, operating on the edge of extinction, any profit shared by the crew—how could he have refused?

"There were three of us," continued the engineer. "Me, Erylin the captain, Chagney the navigator. Too few but we had no choice. We were less later." He doubled in a fit of coughing. "The Rift—damn the luck. Damn it all to hell!"

"What happened?"

"They vanished. They simply vanished. Three men disappearing from a ship in flight. They must have died. Maybe they had a fight or something and the survivor threw out the bodies and himself after them. I don't know. We were going to report it but Chagney advised against it. He acted odd. Kept drinking though he knew it was bad for him. Erylin tried to warn him but nothing he said made any difference. Not him nor me." He coughed again, blood staining the phlegm he spat from his mouth. "Damn the luck. We needed a navigator."

"In the Rift?"

"Where else? How the hell can you hope to navigate without one? Erylin tried but he'd forgotten his skill. The instruments were acting up, old, rotten, the whole stinking ship was rotten. I should have gone with it. Died while I was still whole. Quit like Chagney did—at least he had guts. Jumped out after we left Zakym. Just walked through the port and breathed vacuum. There are worse ways to go."

Lying cooped in a small compartment with a mesh of wire singing with trapped energies—electronic spiders leaping with scintillant darts of flame and no certainty that rescue would ever come. Eking out the food, the water, lying in filth, the body rotting with accelerated decay. Waiting while quick-time compressed days into minutes, the drug altering and slowing the metabolism and so extending life. A convenience which reduced the tedium of long journeys. One used by the engineer to extend his life. One which ended as the cyber watched.

Fralde was a bleak world; the suite given over for the use of Ardoch was little better than the harsh wards of the hospital and differed from a prison only in that the doors were open and the windows unbarred. The Spartan conditions meant nothing to the cyber. A desk at which to work and a chair on which to sit were the only essentials and, in the room to which he retired, a narrow cot was all he asked.

Now he moved toward it, giving the attendant acolyte a single command.

"Total seal. I am not to be disturbed."

As the youth bowed he closed the door on the inner chamber and touched the thick band of metal embracing his left wrist. Electronic energies streamed from the activated mechanism to form a zone through which no spying eye or ear could penetrate. His privacy assured, Ardoch turned to the bed and lay supine, relaxing, breathing regularly as, closing his eyes, he concentrated on the Samatchazi formula. Gradually he lost the use of his senses. He became deaf and, had he opened his eyes, he would have been blind. Divorced of the irritation of external stimuli his mind gained tranquility, became a thing of pure intellect, its reasoning awareness the only thread with reality. Only then did the grafted Homochon elements rise from quiescence.

Rapport was established.

Ardoch became wholly alive.

He soared like a bird and yet more than a bird, flying through vast immensities by the sheer application of thought, gliding past pendants of shimmering crystal, seeing gleaming rainbows locked in an incredible complexity; arching bridges, bows, segments of multi-dimensional circles, lines which turned to twist and turn again so that the entire universe was filled with a coruscating, burning, resplendent effulgence of light which was the essence of truth.

And, at the heart of it, an incredible flower of brilliance among an incredible skein of luminescence, was the convoluted node which was the headquarters of the Cyclan. A fortress buried deep beneath miles of rock and containing the mass of interlocked brains which was the Central Intelligence. The heart of the Cyclan. The multiple brain to which he was drawn, his own intelligence touching it, being absorbed by it, his knowledge sucked into it as dew into arid ground.

Instantaneous organic transmission against which the speed of light was a veritable crawl.

"Dumarest alive! Explain in detail!" Ardoch felt the pulse, the urgency, the determination. *"Are you certain?"*

The engineer had not lied, of that he was convinced. And there was verification. Broge had found Dumarest, had taken him, was on his way to a rendevous in the *Sleethan*. He had communicated and was confident that nothing could go wrong. Too confident for that was the last communication received. Had he been alive he would have established rapport—as he hadn't, it was logical to assume he was dead.

"The engineer was genuine?"

Affirmative.

"And he stated the party had vanished?" A pause. *"From the ship and Dumarest must have been the cause. Even if he had died his body would have been delivered. He destroyed the cyber and his acolyte, evicted them and after?"*

A split second in which countless brains assessed all

possibilities, discarded the impossible, isolated the most probable and produced the answers.

The affinity twin. The secret Dumarest held and for which the Cyclan searched. For which they would hunt him over a thousand worlds and through endless parsecs. Had hunted him and would hunt him still, using every resource to gain the correct sequence in which the fifteen molecular units had to be joined in order to form the artificial symbiote which would ensure the Cyclan the complete and utter domination of the galaxy.

Fifteen biological molecular units, the last reversed to form a subjective half. Injected into a host it settled in the cortex and meshed with the motor and nervous system transmitting all sensory data to the dominant portion. In effect the person carrying it became other than himself. He became the host, living in the body, looking through the eyes, feeling, tasting, sensing—enjoying all the attributes of a completely new body.

An old man could become young again in a firm, virile body. A crone could know the admiration of men and look into a mirror and see the stolen beauty which was hers. A cyber could take over a person of influence and work him as a puppeteer would a marionette. And what one cyber could do so could others. They would occupy every place of power and wealth, each throne, every command.

A secret thought lost when Brasque had stolen it. Thought lost again when every sign pointed to Dumarest having died together with Broge and his acolyte when the *Sleethan* had been lost. As it had been lost, wrecked in the Rift, only the wildest chance bringing it and its sole survivor to light.

"Verification?"

Surely a test, the Central Intelligence did not need the calculations of a lone cyber to check its findings but already it had taken the prediction from Ardoch's brain.

"Probability is in order of ninety-three percent that you are correct. Dumarest must have chosen a crew member to be the host which is the only logical step he could have taken in order to ensure his own survival and arrange for the disappearance. Which?"

A name.

"Correct. It had to be the navigator, Chagney. After the

*ship had deposited its cargo on Zakym the man had to die
in order to release Dumarest's intelligence. Therefore the
excessive drinking. Therefore the apparent suicide."*

A question.

*"Yes. Dumarest must have landed on Zakym hidden in
a box of cargo. The probability is that he is still on that
world. There are unusual attributes to the planet which
would have had a peculiar effect on him. Certainly is lack-
ing but the prediction is eighty-two percent that he is, or
was while on that world, not wholly sane."*

A query.

*"Correction. Sane is not wholly appropriate. He will be
a little abnormal. You will proceed to Zakym with the utmost dispatch. Dumarest is not to be killed or his life or
intelligence placed in danger. This is of utmost priority.
Once found he is to be removed from the planet immediately. That is if he is on Zakym as the prediction implies.
If not he must be followed."*

Acknowledgement and, again, a question.

*"No. Do not hold him and wait for contact by our
agents. Zakym is approaching a critical state as regards the
stability of the present culture. Information from Ilyard
and other worlds shows the interest of mercenary bands.
Find Dumarest and move him before he becomes em-
broiled in a war!"*

The rest was sheer euphoria.

Always, after rapport had been broken, was a period
when the Homochon elements sank back into quiescence
and the mind began to realign itself with the machinery of
the body. Ardoch hovered in a dark immensity, a naked
intelligence untrammeled and unconfined by the limita-
tions of the flesh, sensing strange memories and alien situ-
ations, knowing things he could have never learned, living
lives which could never have been his. A flood of experience, the shards and overflow of other minds, the contact
of other intelligences.

The radiated power of Central Intelligence which filled
the universe with the emitted power of its massed minds.

One day he would become a living part of that tremendous complex. His body would age and reach the end of
its useful life but his mind would remain as sharp and as
active as ever. Then he would be taken, his brain removed

from his skull, placed in a vat of nutrient fluids, connected to a life support apparatus and then, finally, connected to the others, his brain hooked into series with the rest.

He would become a part of Central Intelligence and, at the same time, the whole of it. His ego merging with, absorbed by, assimilating the rest in one total unification.

Converted into a section of an organic computer working continuously to solve each and every secret of the universe. To meld all the races of mankind into a unified whole. To make the Cyclan supreme throughout the galaxy. The aim and object of his being.

Chapter SEVEN

Mbom Chelhar lifted his goblet, studied the engraving, tapped his nail against the edge and, as the thin, clear note died into silence said, "Surely this is not of local manufacture?"

"An import." Lavinia filled the goblet with wine from the decanter she held. "This also. From Ieldhara."

"An interesting world." Chelhar sipped with the fastidiousness of a cat. "Mostly desert but there are fossil deposits to the north together with a high proportion of potash in beds to the south. A combination which lends itself to the production of glass. Have you been there, my lord?"

"Once." Roland selected a fruit and began to remove the peel with a silver knife. "I travelled a little when young and visited most of the Rift-worlds. Do you know it, Earl?"

"No."

"But you have travelled, surely? You have the look of a man who has seen many worlds." Chelhar leaned back in his chair, his eyes lifting to study the groined roof of the hall, the carvings gracing the stone of the walls. "Finally to find a haven, yes? I envy you. Few men have such good fortune."

He was too brash, too forceful and Dumarest wondered why. Lavinia had suggested inviting the man to dinner and he had made no objection; a meal was a good way to gauge the depths of a man when, lulled by food and wine, he felt safe to relax. Roland had joined them, now he rose, dropping the remains of his fruit on the table as he dipped his hands into a bowl of scented water.

"Lavinia, you must excuse me, there are matters demanding my attention. Earl? Chelhar? We shall meet again and soon, I trust."

"Naturally." The man rose, towering above the other by over a head. A tall man, almost as tall as Dumarest and taller than Lavinia who was tall for her race. "You will return home, now?"

"Roland has a suite in the castle." Lavinia touched a bell summoning a servant to clear away the dishes. "In any case he has to stay. Curfew has sounded."

"Of course. Curfew. I had forgotten."

There was irony in his tones and Dumarest watched from where he sat in his chair, noting the play of light over the ebon features, the shape of nose, mouth and jaw. With caste-marks he would have been taken for a Hausi but the cheeks were smooth and there was a subtle difference in the slant of the eyes. A kindred race, perhaps, or somone who carried the stamp of a common ancestry. A dealer who need not be what he seemed.

"You were most gracious to invite me to share your meal," he said. "I appreciate the hospitality and can only regret that we have not met earlier. But I have been busy, you understand. And, always it seems, I get trapped by the curfew." His smile widened. "I think I should introduce the habit on my home world. It has advantages."

"Such as?"

"My lady, I do not care to embarrass you. It is enough to say that the ladies on my planet are somewhat stilted in their conduct toward men and social intercourse is difficult. But if we had a curfew which froze all movement after dark—what an excuse that would be!"

"Your world," said Dumarest. "Tyrahmen?"

"Tyumen," corrected Chelhar. "The names sound similar, I agree, but such error could lead to confusion. My home world lies beyond the Rift towards the Center. Yours?"

"Somewhere." Dumarest poured himself wine, added water, gulped the goblet empty. Lavinia glanced at him as he refilled it, this time with water alone. He was drinking too deeply and too often as if assailed by an unquenchable thirst. "One day I shall return to it."

"Show me the traveller who does not say that!" Chelhar lifted both hands, eyes turning upwards in a parody of prayer. "Always it is 'one day' . . . 'one day' . . . never does it seem to be tomorrow. Strange is it not how the world we remember with such tenderness was the one we were so eager to leave? Like a man I knew once who had a wife who was the most beautiful thing in creation if he was to be believed. Always he praised her but always he remained at a distance. Once, when he had drunk more than he should, I asked him why he stayed away. Can you guess what he answered?"

"No," said Lavinia. "What?"

"My lady, he said that the memory was sweeter than the reality. That to see her would be to spoil his illusion. But, at least, that man was honest with himself. Too many other are not."

"Are you?"

"I have no illusions, my lady. One day I shall return to my world but not until I have made enough money to live as I would like." Chelhar tapped his nail against the rim of his goblet as if to provide an accompaniment to his words. "At times I pray that it will not be long. There are worse planets than Tyumen. We have seas and plains and mountains tipped with snow. The skies are blue and the clouds are white and, at night, a great silver moon adorns the stars. It is old and scarred so that, with imagination, you can see a face looking down at you. Lovers find it pleasant to stroll in its light."

Earth? The man could have been describing Earth—but how many planets had a single moon? A coincidence if not a deliberate trap. But why should a dealer want to set a snare?

Then Chelhar said, softly, "Moonlight. How could you understand its magic? Sunlight, polarized and reflected but somehow magically changed so that the mundane takes on the aspect of mystery and enchantment. Moonlight and starlight, the glory of the heavens, and yet you of Zakym want none of it."

"Can have none of it," corrected Lavinia. "The curfew—"

"Close the door of your prison of night." Chelhar shrugged. "I am in no position to question the local customs or beliefs of any world, but this is one of the strangest. Yes, I know about the Pact and the Sungari, but

I've also heard about ghosts and goblins and things which lurk in the mist. Superstitions which have grown to control the minds and habits of men and peoples. On Angku, for example, no woman may be seen with a naked face. All wear masks and some are fantastic in their depictions; birds, beasts, reptiles, insects, some are things of horror. Yet those same women are forbidden to cover their breasts. Odd, is it not?"

"An original belief or cultural eccentricity," said Lavinia. "But the Sungari are real."

"Of course."

"They exist!" Dumarest had not liked the glance, the hint of a sneer, the smooth manner of a man who was a guest but who seemed to have his own ideas as to how he should conduct himself. "I know."

Chelhar insisted on arguing. "Are you saying that the Sungari actually and literally rule the night? That if I left this castle now, before dawn, they would kill me?"

"Something would destroy you. You would not live to see the dawn." Dumarest halted his hand as it reached for the goblet. "If you wish to put it to the test it can be arranged."

"You would permit me to leave?"

"You spoke of a prison of the night," said Dumarest. "Every house on Zakym is such a prison but I am not your jailer. Leave if you want."

"And die?"

Dumarest picked up his wine. "Yes," he said, flatly. "And die."

The day broke clear, the wreaths of night-mist which had gathered during the night already dissipated in the crips, cool air. Lavinia had chosen to ride and was in the lead, the hooves of her mount ringing against the packed stone of the road, softening to a drumming beat as she led the way to a dirt path which wound up and around the point known as Ellman's Rest.

Dumarest glanced at it as he passed, seeing the gnarled old tree in whose branches a dead man sat and talked at times; a suicide who returned during delusia to warn others against the end he had chosen. Rocks were heaped at the base of the trunk and some night-mist, lingering in the protected shade, hung like wisps of gossamer.

Chelhar turned in his saddle, smiling, and pointed at the lace-like stuff with his whip.

"Food for your mysterious Sungari, Earl? It seems they had little appetite last night."

He smiled, impeccable in his clothing, rich fabrics adorned with gilded thread. His hands were bare, heavy with rings, the nails smooth and neatly rounded. His spurs were rounds of metal rimmed with blunted spikes.

As Dumarest made no answer he said, "I am irritating you, my friend, and for that I apologize. For the informality also if it should offend. I ask you to be generous with my failings—last night we drank deeper than was wise."

Deep, but not too deep for caution and Dumarest wondered if they both had played the same game. As Lavinia had talked enthusiastically about her herd, the dealer making appropriate noises, he had watched with casual attention. Did the man lift his goblet too often and drink too deeply for the amount of wine it contained? Were his gestures a little too wide, his speech a little too hurried? Once he had risen and stumbled as he had crossed the floor and once his hand, as if by accident, had knocked over a glass. Had he pretended to be fuddled?

An old trick for one in his profession but others who dealt in more lethal business could have adopted the same camouflage. As the man rode ahead Dumarest brooded over what he had heard. A ship found drifting in the Rift—the *Sleethan*? The news was old now, the man found would have talked had he been able. It could only have been the captain or the engineer but either, if questioned, would have said too much for his safety. The trail he had thought safely buried would be clear to any with the intelligence to see. And Dumarest had no doubt as to who that would be.

"A fine day, Earl." Roland had ridden to his side. Behind them attendants conveyed mounts loaded with packs; bales of meats and wines for the midday meal which Lavinia intended to make a social occasion. A raft would have provided better transportation but the vehicle would have frightened the beasts. "Comfortable?"

"I can manage."

"Of course. I didn't mean—" Roland broke off, flustered. Rising in his stirrups he looked back, then ahead to where Chelhar was riding close at Lavinia's side. "I'd better join them. There are things I want to say to her in private. Perhaps you would engage the dealer for me, Earl?"

He was being discreet and offering an opportunity to break up the couple. A mark of his jealousy or he could have genuinely had something to tell the woman. Dumarest watched him ride ahead then urged his own mount to a faster pace. Chelhar pulled to one side and waited for him to catch up.

"The Lord Acrae tells me you have the gambler's spirit, my friend. Shall we have a wager? Ten eldrens that I reach the clump of shrub at the edge of the foothills before you. A bet?"

One he couldn't lose. The man rode as well as Lavinia and Dumarest knew himself to be hopelessly outclassed. Chelhar shrugged as, bluntly, he refused.

"I understand. No man wants to appear less than his best before his lady. But we must do something to beguile the journey. For the fun of it, then. I will give you a start. Ride ahead and, when you reach that heap of yellow boulders to the left, I will follow and do my best to win."

Nodding Dumarest touched his heels to the flanks of his mount. The animal started a little, felt the firmness of the hands on the reins and stretched its legs into a gallop. Dumarest, riding with lengthened stirrups, standing so as to clear the jouncing of the saddle, watched as the ground streamed past. He would lose, that was certain, but he would not lose by much. His manner of riding, learned while on Ebth, made for comfort but not for continued bursts of speed. The dealer would win.

But Chelhar was slow in catching up.

Turning Dumarest saw him as he urged on his mount, lying low over the saddle, body rising and falling in perfect synchronization with the movements of the beast. As the patch of scrub came nearer he could hear the thud of hooves, the creak of leather, the pant of the animal's breath.

"Earl!" Lavinia called, waving as she rose in her saddle. "Wait, Earl! Wait!"

Her voice was thin, barely heard over the thud of

hooves, the rush of wind, but Dumarest slowed a little, swinging his mount to the side as Chelhar came up level. The man turned, smiling, teeth flashing against the ebon of his skin, eyes bright beneath the curved line of his brows.

"Fifty eldrens if you catch me, Earl. We are almost at the scrub. Fifty—"

"No."

"Then follow me if you can!"

A stupid challenge, one born of the excitement of the moment and belonging more to a juvenile academy than to the world of grown men. Dumarest slowed even more as the other lunged ahead. He saw Chelhar reach the scrub, vanish into the patch of vegetation and heard again Lavinia's call.

"Stop him, Earl! There are crevasses—broken ground—stop him!"

A man galloping into the unknown, risking his life and that of his mount—for what?

And why?

Dumarest slowed to a walk and edged into the growth. Bushes lay ahead, broken by the passage of the other beast, leaves and broken twigs strewing the ground. Beyond lay a slope scored with shallow gulleys, deeper slashes invisible until reached. A blur of movement revealed Chelhar as he urged his mount up a slope. At the crest he turned, waved, vanished from sight as he plunged down the other side.

Dumarest heard the scrabble of hooves, the ring of metal against rock, the shout and then, rising above all, the ghastly sound of the animal's scream.

It was lying at the bottom of a gully, legs kicking, head rearing, eyes suffused with blood. More blood lay thick around the intestines which bulged from its ripped stomach. Jagged stone, now smeared with carmine, showed where it had hit on the way down, tearing open its belly and breaking its back. Leaving it to kick and scream in helpless agony.

Chelhar lay limp and silent on the edge, a patch of bright color against the drab stone. One hand was thrown out to reveal the empty palm the other, equally empty, lay at his side. He appeared unconscious. He was also un-armed.

The crippled animal screamed again and Dumarest urged his own mount away from the edge. Dropping over the rim he slid down to a narrow ledge, moved along it, dropped again and, slipping, sliding, braking himself with hands and boots, skidded down the steep slope to the bottom of the gully.

The animal reared as he approached, catching his scent, realizing, perhaps, what he intended to do. A man might have been grateful but a beast knew only the need to survive, the drive to avoid extinction. It snapped as Dumarest knelt behind the head, catching it, holding it as, with one quick movement, he plunged his knife into the throat and sent the edge to slice the pulsing artery carrying blood to the brain.

An act of mercy which showered him with blood from the fountain gushing from the wound. A time in which he held the dying beast, easing its pain, giving it what comfort he could. Only when the eyes dulled and the head sagged did he rise, wiping the blade on the dappled hide, thrusting it back into his boot.

Turning he saw Chelhar.

The man had descended the wall of the gully with the agility of a cat, picking his path and drifting down as soundless as a falling leaf. Now he stood, watching, shaking his head as Dumarest stepped from the dead beast.

"A pity, Earl. That was a fine animal."

"It's cost will be put on your account."

"Am I responsible for its death?" The shrug was expressive. "It started, threw me, jumped for some reason and fell. Something must have alarmed it. Almost it killed me—and you want me to pay?"

"Not I—the Lady Lavinia. It was her animal."

"But what is hers is yours, is it not?" The dealer's smile was expressive. "I know the situation, my friend, there are those who have no love for it and they are loose with their mouths at times. How did it happen? A jaded woman, an engrossing stranger—well, such things are common. But do they last, my friend? Have you thought of that? And when the novelty has died—what then?"

Dumarest looked at the man, past him, eyes lifting to

study the edge of the gully, seeing nothing but the glowing light of the twin suns. Magenta and violet which blended to cast a strange, eerie light in this shadowed place.

"You do not answer." Chelhar stepped forward, his right hand lifting, fingers extending as if he intended dropping his hand on Dumarest's shoulder. On the index finger the polished mound of the stone set in the wide band of a ring glowed like a lambent eye.

Glowed and dissolved as something spat from it in a winking thread of flame.

A dart which hummed and sang with a thin, shrilling vibration which grated at the nerves and created a blur of distortion in the air.

One which thudded home in the sleeve of Dumarest's tunic as he flung his left arm upwards to protect his face.

Hitting it drilled; the plastic fuming into smoke, the protective metal mesh beneath fusing to rise in searing vapor, the flesh it covered bursting, pulping, oozing into slime.

Dumarest felt it as his right hand snatched the knife from his boot, sent it slashing upward to rip the dart from its seat, to hurl it to one side where, smoking, it vented the last of its energy on the stone. Another had followed, hitting the tunic where it covered the stomach, falling as again the knife jerked it free.

"Fast!" Chelhar backed, his hand rising to his mouth, eyes wide with disbelief. "I heard you were fast but never dreamed you could move so quickly. I—"

He died as the knife spun through the air to hit, to drive its point into the soft flesh of the throat, to sever arteries and to finally lodge in the spine. A death too quick, too merciful—but Dumarest had had no choice.

He swayed a little as he looked down at the dead man. His arm, and stomach bore pits of disrupted tissue. The fingers of the hand which had held the knife were bruised, the nails oozing blood, cells ruptured by the transmitted vibrations of the darts. The ring from which they had spat was empty now but Chelhar wore other rings, some as harmless diversions but at least one other must be carrying a lethal device.

It was on his other hand, the one he had been lifting to his mouth when, by talk, he had hoped to engage his intended victim's attention. An assassin's trick. One which had failed.

Dumarest looked at the walls of the gully. For an active, agile man they presented no real obstacle but he was hurt and knew he could never climb them. The darts had done more than disrupt tissue; toxins had been formed which even now were poisoning his blood and affecting his senses. To shout would be to waste time as no one was within earshot. His mount could have been found but a search for its rider would take time.

He moved, stepping over the body, heading to one end of the gully where a wider patch of sky could be seen. The sides would be less steep there, the chances greater of finding an easy path. Then he halted, remembering, wondering why it had taken him so long to think of a better way.

To try to climb would be to accelerate the action of the toxins, to shout would be to waste strength, but a fire would send up smoke which would attract any searchers.

He lit one, striking sparks from the back of his knife with a stone, feeding them to fragments of frayed cloth from Chelhar's garments, adding more fuel, forming smoke with fabric dipped in blood. As the bottom of the gully there was no wind, the smoke rose high and straight, spreading only when it rose into the upper air. Even so stray wreaths of it flowered from the blaze and stung his eyes and caught at his lungs. Harsh, acrid fumes which held the stench of roasting tissue. Billows of smoke which veiled the area in a noxious haze.

In it something moved.

Delusia? The suns were too far apart for that. A predator? They were unknown in the Iron Mountains. The Sungari?

Dumarest reared up from where he leaned against the wall of the gully and reached for his knife. It was daylight, the Sungari had no right to appear, by doing so they broke the Pact. Then the creature moved again, a foal which whinnied and ran from the smells and sight of death, leaving Dumarest alone to sit and drift and fall deeper into the pit at the bottom of which death was waiting.

Chapter EIGHT

"You were lucky," said the physician. "But then, without luck, how long would a man like yourself continue to live?"

A question Dumarest didn't bother to answer. He stretched in the bed, feeling the tug of newly healed flesh on arm and stomach. His right hand, when he examined it, was clear of bruises. Aside from hunger and a consuming thirst he felt completely well. Slow-time, of course, the converse of the drug which made long journeys seem short. Beneath its influence his metabolism would have speeded so that he lived hours in a matter of minutes. Kept unconscious his body had healed while he slept.

"You've been under for a week subjective," said the doctor. "I used hormone salves and gave you a complete blood-wash to remove the toxins. Forced growth of injured tissue and, naturally, intravenous feeding. I've had you resting under micro-current induced sleep for a while—I'm not fond of jerking my patients awake directly from slow-time unless there's a good reason. You're hungry, of course."

"And thirsty. Some water?" Dumarest drank, greedily. "Thank you. What happened?"

"You were unconscious when found. I was summoned and fortunately was able to get there in time. I gave you emergency treatment, had you brought into town and here you are." The doctor frowned as Dumarest helped himself to more water. "Do you always have such a thirst?"

"Recently, yes."

"Strongly recurring? By that I mean you drink, wait, feel an intense thirst and then have to drink again. All in short intervals. Too short to be normal. Yes?" His frown deepened as Dumarest nodded. "Any vomiting, signs of nausea, double vision?"

"No. Why?"

"Persistent thirst is a symptom of brain damage. A symptom, mind, not conclusive evidence that such damage exists. Coupled with difficulty in moving and a general torpor it could signal a lesion in the base of the brain." His eyes narrowed at Dumarest's sudden tension. "Is anything wrong?"

"No. Can you test for such damage?"

"Of course. If you wish I'll make an appointment for you to come in later."

"Now." Dumarest threw his legs over the edge of the cot and sat upright. He wore only a thin hospital gown. Rising he felt a momentary nausea which was the natural result of a body which had rested too long and had been too quickly moved. "I want you to do it now."

As the doctor readied his instruments there was time for thought. The dominant half of the affinity twin which he had injected into himself had nestled at the base of the cortex. When Chagney had died it should have dissolved and been assimilated into his metabolism. But—if Chagney had not died?

The concept was ridiculous. He had forced the body to step into space. He had seen through the borrowed eyes the naked glory of the universe. Had felt them burst, the lungs expand, the tissue yield to the vacuum. All had died, brain, bone, body—all dehydrated in the emptiness of the void, drifting now and for always in the vast immensity of space.

Dead.

Totally erased.

Then why did he continue to hear the crying? The thin, pitiful wailing of a creature trapped and helpless and knowing he was to die?

"Are you all right?" The doctor was standing before him, leaning forward over the chair, his eyes anxious. "Here!" His hand lifted bearing a vial, pungent vapors rising from the container to sting eyes and nostrils. "Inhale deeply. Deeply."

Dumarest pushed it aside. "Doctor, how long can a brain live?"

"Without oxygen about three minutes. After that time degeneration of tissue begins to set in and any later recovery will be attended by loss of function."

"And if it could be preserved in some way? Frozen, for example?"

"As it is when you travel Low?" The doctor pursed his lips. "Theoretically, in such a case, life is indefinite. In actual practice the slow wastage of body tissue will result in final physical breakdown and resultant death. I believe, on Dzhya, they have criminals who have lain in the crytoriums for two centuries and who still register cerebral activity on a subconscious level. In theory, if a brain could be thrown into stasis, residual life would remain."

In a brain suddenly exposed to the vacuum of space? One dehydrated and frozen before any cellular disruption could have taken place?

Was the subjective half of the affinity twin still alive?

"You're sweating," said the doctor. "You don't have to be afraid."

Not of the machines and instruments ringing the chair but there was more. Was he still connected to Chagney? Would he continue to hear the man crying? Had he locked himself into a prison from which there could be no escape?

How to find a drifting body in the void? How to destroy it?

"Steady," said the doctor. "Just relax and close your eyes. I want to insert a probe and take some measurements. Just think of something pleasant."

A dead man drifting, ruptured eyes scars in the mask of his face, blood rimming his mouth with a long-dried crust, his heart a lump of tissue, stomach puffed, lungs a ruin— but his brain? His mind? The thing it contained?

"Easy," said the doctor. "Easy."

A probe silling into his mind. Dumarest could imagine it, the slender tool plunging deep, touching the artificial symbiote nestling at the base of the cortex, stimulating it, perhaps, building a strengthened bond with its other half.

Would his mind fly to that other body? Live again in dead and frozen tissue? Know nothing but the silent emptiness, the unfeeling void?

A chance, but a risk which had to be taken. He had to know.

"Steady!" The doctor drew in his breath. "There!" He let the moment hang as he checked the withdrawn probe and studied the findings. "Nothing. The scan shows no trace of a tumor and no excessive pressure. There is no scarring and no malformation. There is however a trace of an unusual compactness of tissue at the base of the cortex as if there was a slight concentration of molecular structure. Biologically it is nothing to worry about. It may barely, have given rise to your increased thirst but I tend to think the cause is more psychological than physical."

"How so?"

"As you know Zakym is an unusual world. Some adapt and some do not. A few find it too disturbing to live here for long. There is a breakdown in the adaption syndrome which reveals itself in unusual physical oddities. One man, I remember, developed a tormenting itch while another acquired a craving for salt. If the thirst continues I would be tempted to look for the reason in the psychosomatic region. You are in excellent physical condition and you most certainly have nothing to worry about as regards the organic health of your brain."

"Thank you," said Dumarest.

"For giving you reassurance?"

"For saving my life. The bill?"

"Lady Lavinia has taken care of that. She left word she would be waiting for you at the hotel."

It was night and Dumarest made his way through the maze of tunnels connecting the various buildings of the town. A corridor led to the hotel and he climbed stairs leading to snugly shuttered chambers. Lavinia was in the common room seated at a table. She was not alone.

"Earl!" She rose as she saw him and came to meet him, smiling, hands extended. They lifted to fall to his shoulders as, without hesitation, she pressed herself close, her lips finding his own. "Thank God you are well! The doctor—"

"Gave me a clean bill of health." Holding her he added, quietly, "You saved me."

"You saved yourself. We saw the smoke and found you

and I had men ride back to summon the physician and get a raft. Roland helped. Chelhar—Earl, what happened?"

"A mistake." One which had cost the assassin his life but this was not the time or place to talk about it. Dumarest glanced at the man seated at the table. "A friend of yours?"

"Not of mine, of yours. Don't you recognize him? Kars Gartok. He arrived this afternoon Ilyard. He claims to have known you for years."

He rose as they approached the table, his scarred face creasing into a smile. His bow was deferential without being obsequious. A man accustomed to dealing with the rich and powerful but one who had retained his independence.

He tensed as Dumarest strode towards him, seeing the eyes, the anger they held, the set of the mouth which had grown cruel. A killer's mask. Quickly he lifted both hands and held them before him. The fingers were devoid of rings.

"I am unarmed!"

"And a liar!"

"There are times when need dictates deception. You were unavailable." He glanced at the woman. "My lady I apologize for my subterfuge yet I did not wholly lie. While not close we do have mutual acquaintances if not exactly friends. Major Kan Lofoten, for example? You remember him, Earl?"

Dumarest met the deep-set eyes, his own shifting to the temples, the scars, the corners of the mouth, recognizing the choice the man had given him by the use of his name. He could reject it and learn nothing.

"Hoghan," he said. "You were there?"

"A bad world and a bad war. Yes, Earl, I was on Hoghan fighting under Atlmar."

"And Lofoten?"

"Dead with most of the Legion. Chelha—all plagues are a curse, of them all chelha is most to be feared. I was lucky and managed to escape in time. Well, enough of that, some things are best forgotten." Gartok glanced at the bottle standing on the table. "Are best drowned in wine. Of your charity, my lady?"

She smiled at the quaint method of asking for a drink. "You need no charity."

"You are gracious." Gartok lifted the bottle. "You will join me, Earl?"

Dumarest nodded, watched as the man poured, lifted his glass and studied the other over the rim. A man typical of his type but with a gift the majority lacked. A touch of humor, a philosophical attitude towards the life he had chosen, a native shrewdness which had enabled him to survive. A man who had sought him out—why?

"To warn you," he said when Dumarest asked the question. "You are a target, my friend. Need I say more?"

"A target?" Lavinia didn't understand then, as the meaning dawned on her, she caught her breath. "An assassin? Earl!"

"His name?"

"How can I answer that? Men use many names, my friend, but watch for a stranger who has an excuse for getting close. Someone not too—" Gartok broke off, his eyes narrowing. "Am I too late?"

"Chelhar!" Lavinia's glass broke in her hand. "Mbom Chelhar!"

A man who had been a little too eager, a little too inexperienced and so had made the lethal mistake of underestimating his victim. His casual disregard of protocol, the lack of elementary courtesy, his challenge, his very attitude had jarred with his adopted pose. Now he was dead and his secrets with him.

Dumarest said, "How did you know I was a target?"

"Rumors. Whispers in the dark. Hints dropped over wine—does it matter?"

"It matters. You mentioned Hoghan. I never saw you there. You fought under Haiten, you say?"

"Haiten lost. I was with Atlmar." Gartok reached for the bottle and poured himself more wine. "And we never met—did I claim we had? I learned of you from a captain who was greatly impressed. Listening to him I gained the impression that you watched a soldier lift his rifle, waited until he had fired then dodged the bullet. An exaggeration, naturally, but stories gain in the telling. And later I saw you as you walked in the town." He glanced at Lavinia. "You were not alone."

"A woman, Earl?" Lavinia had caught the subtle shift of inflexion. "Were you with a woman?"

Looking at the mercenary Dumarest said, "Describe her."

"Tall, well-made, beautiful if your interests lie in the patrician mold. She had red hair and her nails were tipped with metal. Her name—"

"I know her name." The man was either well-schooled or telling the truth. "Why are you here?"

"I told you. To carry a warning." Gartok stared at Dumarest for a long moment, then sighed. "There is more, naturally. Sometimes in life a man recognizes an opportunity. If he is wise he takes it. And, if others aid him in his ambition, well, what else can he do but follow the tide? On Ilyard I heard rumors of the situation here on Zakym. Of an heir eager to claim his inheritance—or a man claiming to be that heir. You see the difference?"

"Go on."

"There was a monk who died. An old man but tough as monks always are. Why should he have died? I was curious and went to his cremation. I saw there a man with his wife and both seemed unduly distressed. The woman was almost hysterical. Again I wondered why she should have been so upset at the death of an old man. So I investigated and found something, an old book which the monk had kept. A record of sorts. I borrowed it."

"And?"

"I will make it plain, my friend. Gydapen had a partner as surely you must have guessed. His name is Charl Embris and he is one of the largest dealers on Ilyard. You want men, guns, heavy equipment in order to wage a war? He can supply them. Credit? He can supply that too. Offer him the loot of a world and the prospect will fill his universe." Gartok drained the last of his wine then added, quietly, "You can appreciate why such a man would be your enemy."

"He sent the assassin?"

"Yes."

"And the monk?" Lavinia leaned forward over the table. "What had he to do with it?"

"Nothing. He was a victim and that was all. Lady Othurine, Embris's wife, was distraught and sought comfort from the church. The old monk attended her. She would have told him things others wanted to remain secret. Her husband for one. Her son for another. Especially her son."

"The false heir?"

"You are shrewd, my lady. When Gydapen died an excuse had to be found to continue with the original plan. The original heir provided it. He is dead, of course, and his identity has been adopted by another. A vicious murder for the sake of greed, but what intelligent man would set another on a throne when he could take it for himself? The Lady Othurine loved her son and is afraid for him. She spoke of this to the old monk." Gartok stared into his empty glass. "For that he died."

Assassinated in order to close his mouth. Such things were easily arranged on a world devoted to the pursuit of war.

But the mercenary—where did his interests lie?

"You mentioned a book," said Dumarest. "Which you borrowed."

"And which the monks reclaimed. The Church abhors violence, Earl, but justice is another matter. We came to an arrangement. Armed with knowledge they had given me I visited Embris and came to an understanding. He thinks I am here on his behalf."

"Are you?"

Gartok lifted his glass and turned it in his thick fingers, a single drop of wine moving sluggishly over the crystal; blood won from a reluctant wound.

"I am a gambler, Earl, what else can a mercenary be? To work for Embris is to work for the man who hopes to make this world his own and for what? Small pay and high risk and, when the prize has been won, scant thanks and small reward. Now, if I were to work with you. . . ?" He let his voice trail into silence.

"I have nothing, you realize that?"

"You have yourself."

Lavinia said, sharply, "What do you hope to gain?"

"Money, my lady." Gartok was blunt. "A high place, lands, certainly rich compensation—all conditional on victory. If we lose I get nothing."

"If we lose Earl could be dead!"

A prospect which tormented her and one she mentioned when, later, they were alone. The room was one of the best the hotel could provide, the light soft amber from lanterns of tinted glass, the floor thick with woven rugs. Sitting on the edge of the wide, soft bed she looked at him, noting the way he moved, the calm, contained energy he radiated, the determination.

"Earl, what would I do without you?"

"You'd live."

"How can you say that? Before I met you life was just an existence. Now——?" She broke off, knowing she needed to be strong, wondering why she was not. To yield to a man, to rely on him was to become weak and yet it was nice to be comforted by his strength, to rest warm in the assurance that she was not alone. "Can we trust him?"

"Gartok?" He frowned. "I think so."

"We could make certain," she suggested. "There are tests—no?"

"No."

She didn't ask him to explain, to point out that a man of Gartok's stamp had his honor such as it was and that to demand tests was to offer insult. And, had the man been conditioned, available tests would prove nothing. Instead she said, with acid jealousy, "That woman he mentioned. The one you were with on Hoghan. You didn't let him mention her name."

"Dephine."

"Just that?" Her tone made it plain what she thought. "A harlot?"

"A woman who is dead now."

"Dead?" She smiled then grew serious. "Like the others, Earl? The ones you see at delusia? Kalin and Derai and the one you thought I was? Lallia? You remember? All the women who come to talk to you and smile and warn you against me, perhaps. Is that what they do, Earl? Laugh at me? Deride me for loving you!"

"Stop it!"

"Yes." She looked at her hands and made an effort to hold them still. Light caught her nails and was reflected in trembling shimmers. "I am the Lady Lavinia Del Belamosk. A member of the Council of Zakym. I should not be jealous."

"No," he said, flatly. "You shouldn't."

"But, Earl—" She rose and stepped toward him, hands extended for comfort, wanting him to tell her that no other woman had meant anything to him, that only now, with her, had he found love. "Earl, please!"

He said, quietly, "Did life only begin for you, Lavinia, when we met? Am I the only man you have ever known?"

For a moment she made no answer then, drawing in her breath, lowered her hands and managed to smile.

"I'm sorry, Earl. I was being foolish. Before you came to me you didn't exist and nothing you had done could matter. The women you knew—none of them are real to me. They live only in your memory. It was just that I was afraid, thinking of you getting hurt, of dying, even."

"Death is a risk of war."

"Do we have to fight?"

"No." The answer surprised her and he smiled at her expression. "We could yield to all demands made by Gydapen's heir."

"The false heir."

"True or false makes no difference. He is coming with the power to make his claim real. Once he is accepted who will argue as to whose son he really is? Tomir Embris will do as well as any. He will rule. Zakym will become his world. His father will supply the arms and men he needs. There will be a dozen others who would be eager to share in the operation and every unemployed mercenary on Ilyard will hurry to join the feast. If I yield the lands—"

"If?" Her voice carried her shock at the suggestion. "Earl, you can't! You mustn't!"

"Why not?"

"You haven't been paid! Our child must inherit!"

The first reason was enough; a bargain made was a bargain which should be kept and money was necessary for continuing the search for Earth. The second?

Dumarest looked at the woman. Was she pregnant or was the claim a woman's wile? A lie designed to weaken his resolve to hunt for the planet of his birth, to keep him at her side? It was possible, as possible as the claimed pregnancy if his seed was still viable after so many years spent exposed to the radiations of space.

"Our lands, Earl," she said, urgently. "Those of Bela-mosk and Prabang. Together they will make the largest holding on Zakym. We could absorb others, expand, break and cultivate new ground. Grow, Earl. Grow!"

Building chains to hold him, new responsibilities which would claim his attention, a net of need in which to hold him fast. Looking at him Lavinia realized she was going too fast too far. Little by little, step by step, to catch such a man needed care.

"The child you speak of." He was blunt. "Are you pregnant?"

"You doubt me, Earl?"

"I asked a question."

"And received an answer. We of Belamosk do not lie."

And neither did they tell the whole of the truth. No answer had been given and she must know it. Then why the reluctance? Fear of losing him on the first vessel? Fear of his reaction? Fear that what was yet in doubt could turn out to be a false hope?

A trap baited with honey—and what could be sweeter than a baby's need?

"Earl?" She came to him, all warmth and invitation, perfume rising from the mane of her hair, the subtle scents of her body augmenting the selected odor. "Earl, will you fight?"

For Earth. For the money to find it. For the pride of holding what was his own. For the woman and the child she could be carrying and the security both would need.

"Yes," he said. "I'll fight."

Chapter NINE

Castle Belamosk changed. The gentle air of unhurried indolence vanished to be replaced by a fevered sense of urgency with women kept busy sewing uniforms of strong fabric reenforced with leather, with artisans making heavy boots, edged weapons, belts, canteens. Others furbished old weapons; sporting rifles and pistols used in formal duels, even crossbows made to designs supplied by Dumarest.

He shrugged when Lavinia pointed out the primitive nature of the weapons.

"A bolt can kill as surely as a bullet if well-aimed. It would be nice to equip the men with lasers but we haven't got them."

"But crossbows?"

"Are easy to make and simple to use. The bolts they use can be recovered and used again and again. The weapon itself will get them used to the weight of arms." Patiently he ended, "Leave it to me, Lavinia. I know what I'm doing."

Arming and teaching men to be soldiers, to march and drill and to kill when given the order. But, as the days passed, she realized that to train men wasn't as simple as she had thought.

"It's a matter of cultural conditioning," explained Roland when she spoke of it one day after watching a group of young boys try and fail to perform a simple maneuver. "Our retainers have never had to think for themselves in their entire lives. They know what to do and how it should be done and have never had the need to think of alternative methods. Now they are being asked to change their social pattern into something strange and a little frightening. To perform acts without apparent purpose. To obey without apparent need. March, turn, halt, drop, aim,

100

fire—words new to their vocabulary. But don't worry, my
dear, Earl knows what he is doing."

Bran Welos wasn't so sure.

At first it had been a game and he had been eager to
thrust himself forward for, as his dead father had advised
during delusia, the one who was among the first would be
the one to gain rapid advancement. And Gelda had been
pleased and given him the reward of her body that same
night after curfew when the castle had been sealed against
the dark. Even at dawn when he has assembled with the
others it hadn't seemed too hard. The initial marching had
become tiresome and the drills were stupid but there were
watching faces to smile at and familiar things to see.

Then Kars Gartok had struck him and knocked him
down and swore at him as he lay with blood running from
his nose.

"Pay attention you fool! Left is left not right! March,
don't slouch, and take that silly grin off your face. You're
a man, not a clown. Head up, shoulders squared, stomach
in, chest out, back straight, eyes ahead—now on your feet
and march! March! March!"

March until his legs grew weak with fatigue, his feet
sore with blisters, his eyes burning with glare and dust.
March and obey until he had become a machine without
sense or feeling. Then the long, long journey out into the
arid lands without water or food and with the crossbow he
had been given a dragging weight at his shoulder.

"Keep in step there!" Dumarest was in charge of the
party. "Left! Left! Left, right, left! Don't drag your feet!
Left! Left!"

Welos spat and muttered something. Dumarest heard it
but paid no attention. Anger was a good stimulus and if a
man trained to be deferential all his life could have found
the courage to vent his displeasure then it was a sign the
training was having some effect.

A man stumbled, fell, lay in hte dust. He turned to face
the sky, his cracked lips parting.

"Water I must have water!"

"On your feet!"

"A drink! I must—"

"Get up!" Stooping Dumarest lifted the man by brute
force. "You aren't thirsty," he snapped. "You haven't been

out long enough for that. Now suck a pebble or something and stop thinking about water. Just concentrate on putting one foot before the other. March!" His tone became ugly. "March, damn you, or I'll cut your throat!"

One glance at the harsh set of the features and the man hurried to catch up with the rest, thirst and weariness forgotten. As he moved forward Dumarest looked at the sky. The suns were past the zenith, edging close but, he hoped, not too close for delusia. He had enough problems without having the group of men complain to their dead relatives and friends and, perhaps, being given destructive advice.

He halted the column at the summit of a knoll and checked for landmarks and guides.

"Listen." He looked at the ring of attentive faces. "Pay attention. You're all hungry and thirsty and tired and you'd like a chance to rest and take things easy. Right?"

He waited for the murmur of agreement to fade.

"If you were ordinary men you could do that but you are soldiers. Soon you'll have to fight and your lives will depend on your ability to learn. What I want you to realize is that you can go on far longer than you think is possible. You can last without food and water and rest and move faster than you know. We're going to prove it. You!" His finger scanned. "How much further can you walk?"

"A few miles, sir. Maybe three."

"You?"

"Five at least." The man scowled at the murmurs of protest. "I'm not soft like the rest of you. I worked on the land."

And so was relatively tough as those who tended the herd were the toughest of them all, but those men couldn't be spared.

"On your feet!" Dumarest waited then, pointing, said. "Over there lies food and water and huts with beds in which to sleep. Normally it would take a man seven hours of hard walking to cover the distance. It will be dark in six. So, on the double, move!"

The lamp was a glass container filled with oil, an adjustable wick, a chimney of tinted crystal. Kars Gartok lit it, adjusted the flame and set it on the table. Bowls of food stood on the board together with flagons of brackish water and thin wine.

"Three," he said. "You pushed them hard, Earl."

Dumarest leaned back in his chair, lines of fatigue tracing their paths over his face. "Dead?"

"No. Just exhausted, but if we hadn't sent out for them they'd be where they had fallen." He looked at the shuttered windows. "Out on the desert in the dark. They were crying when we found them, sick with fear of the Sungari." Pausing he added, "Would they have died?"

"Yes."

"Of fear or—"

"Not of fear." The wine was tart, refreshing to the heart and Dumarest took some, holding it in his mouth before swallowing. "How are you making out?"

"How would you expect? They handle a gun as if it were a brick? A few have learned how to load, cock and fire and, of those few, some even manage to hit the target. Those who were trained by Gydapen are better."

And were being used to instruct others but even they were short of the standard Dumarest hoped to achieve.

"You can't do it, Earl." Gartok helped himself to wine. "With the best will in the world you can't do it. It's been tried before. On Marat some farmers were being oppressed and formed themselves into a defensive unit. They got hold of weapons and elected a leader. They marched and drilled and learned how to use a gun and hit a target almost every time. They thought they were ready and made their defiance. Need I tell you what happened?"

"They failed?"

"It was a shambles." Gartok gulped at his wine. "They scattered when they should have held their ground, advanced when they should have retreated, fought when they should have waited and waited when they should have gone into action. No skill. No application. Nothing but raw courage and it wasn't enough."

"And?"

"These men you've found don't even have courage. They simply obey because they're used to taking orders. Roland thought that was all we needed. He didn't understand as we do that a good soldier obeys, true, but he uses his own intelligence when carrying out orders to achieve

the maximum benefit from any situation. To listen to the
Lord Acrae you'd think all a commander had to do was to
swamp guns with targets. Amateurs!" He echoed his dis-
gust. "Damned amateurs!"

"Like Tomir?" Dumarest rose as the mercenary stared
at him. "Is he an amateur?"

Gartok frowned. "What do you mean, Earl? He's the
son of a foremost dealer on Ilyard."

"But not a trained and experienced mercenary. Not a
seasoned commander. He's coming with armed men but
what else? Flyers? Heavy equipment? Mobile detach-
ments? Long-range artillery? Field-lasers? How much is
Embris willing to spend? The boy will want a cheap victory in order to prove himself, right?"

"I guess so."

"Don't guess!" Dumarest was sharp. "You're a professional and I want a professional opinion. In Tomir's place
what would you do?"

For a moment the mercenary remained silent then he
said, slowly, "Heavy forces or light—which way will the
cat jump? A wise man would use every man and weapon
he's got and saturate the area. He'd crush all thought of
opposition before it could even get started. But that would
be expensive and so many men could create a problem
later. Embris isn't noted for his extravagance and he has
no way of knowing you intend to oppose him. I'd say Tomir will arrive with a small force and have reenforcements
at hand waiting his call."

A calculated assessment and probably correct.

"And?"

"We could get him when he lands, Earl. Snipers set to
open fire when he appears. A few shots and it will be
over."

"You're not thinking, Kars. Kill him like that and his
father will want revenge—and he wouldn't spare any expense to get it."

"True." Gartok helped himself to more wine, leaning
forward so that the light of the lamp shone strongly on the
seams and scars of his face giving him the momentary appearance of a gargoyle. "What then?"

"We wait for him to attack."

"That's crazy! Why give him the advantage?"

"We have no choice." From a cabinet Dumarest took a folded paper and opened it. The photographs he'd taken had been trimmed, matched, details enhanced and the whole copied to give an aerial view of the area around Belamosk together with that of other holdings. "He's coming to claim Gydapen's land. To attack him before he gets it will be to alienate the Council and to invite retaliation. We'll be giving him an excuse to commence a war. We can't hold both Belamosk and Prabang so Prabang has to go."

"You surrender it?"

"I have to. Now Belamosk will have the only armed force on Zakym aside from Tomir's men. He'll have to attack us first before he can hope to expand. If he doesn't and reaches for other holdings then the Council will appeal to us for help. Either way we shall have right on our side."

"Right?" Gartok was cynical. "That, my friend, belongs to the side with the biggest battalions."

"And the largest rewards to those with the smallest." Dumarest cleared the table with a sweep of his arm and spread out the map. "Assuming Tomir will attack from the direction of Prabang he will raft his men in to this area. Agreed?"

Gartok studied the terrain. "Flat ground and a wide field of view. Close enough to avoid excessive fatigue yet far enough to be safely out of range. A natural choice, Earl. So?"

"If he does then the column must move along this defile and through this pass. We can set up defensive points here and here." Dumarest's finger tapped at spots on the map. "But if their commander is wise he will be expecting an ambush and divert his attack to pass along here. It's the next best route."

"If he follows the book, Earl, yes. It's the classic pattern."

"So we set our men here and here and catch the column in a cross-fire. They'll be cut to pieces before they know what's hit them."

"Maybe." Gartok was doubtful. "I've seen these map-strategies fail before. It's a mistake to rely on them. If Tomir follows the book your plan could work but what makes you think he will?"

"Pride." Dumarest straightened from where he leaned over the map. "He is young and eager to prove himself. He's an amateur but he won't let that stop him. He'll want all the credit and all the glory but, above all, he'll want a quick victory. That's a combination guaranteed to breed mistakes. He'll forget something or overlook something and, when he does, we'll have him."

"So we move to Belamosk?"

"Yes."

"And wait?"

"And wait." Dumarest folded the map. "And get ready to welcome Tomir."

He came in a dozen rafts adorned with bright pennants each vehicle filled with armed and armored men. Dumarest watched them from his place on the summit of a hill, seeing the helmets, the body-armor, the glint of weapons. A show of force designed to intimidate and a little exaggeration to enhance the display. The rafts were not filled to capacity—half the number would have served to move the men, but against the bowl of the sky they looked menacing; shapes of destruction coming to deal death.

A courtesy visit, so Tomir had claimed, but Dumarest knew better. Now, lowering his binoculars, he called to the mounted man standing at the foot of the slope.

"Ride to the summit of knoll 8 and raise the blue standard."

A pre-arranged signal which would keep half his forces hidden, expose a third of the remainder as a diversion and warn Gartok not to hesitate when the rafts came close enough to ensure direct hits.

Turning he studied the castle. The walls were deserted and the great doors closed. Rafts could drop into the courtyard but, if they did, a storm of fire would bathe the area. Tilting his head he looked at the sky. The suns were wide apart and long hours remained of the day. As yet Tomir had planned well.

"Earl?" Gartok was below astride a sweating animal. "I've spotted movement to the east. Ground troops, I think, keeping under cover. The rafts could be a diversion to get us to expose our positions."

A possibility Dumarest had considered. "How far distant are they?"

"A mile or two."

The rafts were closer but moving slowly and keeping high. An aerial reconnaissance? Any good commander would have ordered one but, if the men remained under cover, it would do him little good. The area around the castle was broken stone and arid soil and could hide a small army.

"We could go out and meet them," suggested Gartok. Exchange shots and keep low. It would make them reveal their intention."

"No." Dumarest made his decision. "That's what they want. If they can draw us out they'll learn our numbers and state of our men. As it is they have to guess. We'll keep them guessing. Hold your positions and stay out of sight. Let them come to us. Guerrilla war—you know what to do."

"Hit and run." The mercenary was sour. "Stab in the back. Kill stragglers and those who aren't looking. A hell of a way to fight a war."

"We aren't fighting a war," said Dumarest. "We're trying to stay alive. Now get moving."

Dumarest descended from the summit of the hill as Gartok rode away. Men out riding were to be expected on land used for the breeding of mounts and any watching would see nothing of potential danger. Looking up he saw the rafts had drifted lower. A good sign; if they had been suspicious the vehicles would have been lifted high or landed fast. But the movement could be a diversion to hold the attention from the men Gartok had spotted. And, if he'd seen them, there could be others he had missed.

A classic strategy straight from the book. Divert, decoy, distract—then destroy.

How to break the pattern?

Dumarest looked around, saw a slope of rock facing the direction from which the rafts had come, jagged stone which edged the crest, boulders resting precariously to either side.

Hefting his rifle he moved into the cover.

It was a sporting weapon, the stock decorated in an ornate design, the universal sight showing a ruby dot to mark the impact point of the bullet. The magazine held a score of them each capable of blasting a hole through a brick wall at a thousand yards. The rifle could place all twenty in a half-inch circle at twice that distance.

Dumarest aimed at the leading raft.

It was slightly tilted, the men gathered to one side and leaning over the edge, one pointing at something he had seen below. The hand was replaced by the barrel of a gun, a beam of ruby light guiding the laser blast which followed. From somewhere to one side a man screamed.

Dumarest fired.

The man who held the laser reared, turning, dropping the weapon as he clutched at his upper arm. The visor of his helmet was raised, his face visible, crumpling as a second bullet smashed into the forehead between the eyes.

As he fell Dumarest fired again and again, sending a stream of bullets against the raft. The body-armor the men wore was protection against slow-moving missiles and the reflected beams of lasers but not against the high-velocity ammunition he was using. A direct hit would penetrate and kill.

The raft spun, tilted, turned and sent men falling like tattered leaves to the broken ground beneath.

As Dumarest reloaded, return fire sent chips of stone humming like broken razors through the air.

"Fire! He heard Gartok's roar. "From cover, at the rafts, aim steady and squeeze slow. Get those bastards! Get them!"

Weeks of training now put to the test. If the men broke and tried to run from the return fire they would be mowed down. If they fired wildly all they would do would be to waste ammunition. If they froze they were useless.

"Steady!" Again the mercenary's voice rose above the sound of firing. "Steady, damn you! Aim before you fire! Aim!"

A raft jerked upwards and a man shrieked as he fell, blood showering from his riddled legs. Another, leaning far over the side, slumped as Dumarest sent a bullet into his throat, the laser he was about to use spinning to shatter on a rock. Shifting aim Dumarest fired at the rafts further back, aiming at the engines and hoping to bring them down. One suddenly dropped, levelled, fell again with smoke rising from inside. The others climbed high into the sky.

"Cease fire!" Gartok yelled. "Stay under cover. Check your loads. Any wounded?"

He turned, grinning as Dumarest joined him. Standing in the open he appeared to be alone then Dumarest saw the men lying beneath slabs of stone, huddled in cracks, curled beneath boulders. The air held the stench of burned explosives.

"They held, Earl!" The mercenary gestured around. "They held and they returned the fire!"

"How many hurt?"

"Three dead." Gartok shrugged at Dumarest's expression. "Well, it happens. Twelve with minor injuries, cuts and singes. Four seriously wounded—one the man who started it all."

He lay in a crumpled heap to one side, a young man with wide eyes and hair through which some girl had loved to run her fingers. The laser had caught his arm and stomach, severing the limb and leaving a charred stump, slicing into the abdomen to leave a wound which oozed blood and twisted intestines.

A man already dead but who stubbornly refused to let go.

"He ran," whispered Gartok. "God knows why. He suddenly upped and ran and that bastard in the raft let him have it. Not even a clean kill either. I'm glad you got him, Earl."

Revenge, but what did it matter to the dying man? Dumarest saw his eyes, their movement, the tip of the tongue which touched the lips.

"Get some water."

"For him? With that gut-wound?"

"He's dying, what difference does it make?" Dumarest knelt with the canteen in his hand. Gently he moistened the parched lips, feeling the febrile heat of the cheek, the burning fever which consumed the young man. "Sip a little," he urged. "Easy now. Easy."

"Did we win?"

"We won." A lie, but what did it matter? Frowning Dumarest added, "I know you. Bran Welco, isn't it?"

"Bran Welos, sir. I'm glad you remember me. I was on that march when you almost ran us into the ground. I didn't think I'd make it, but I did." The stump of the charred arm lifted a little as if he wanted to put out his hand. "Why did that man burn me?"

"You ran. Why?"

"I saw my grandfather. He smiled and beckoned to me."

Delusia? Dumarest glanced at the sky and saw the suns still well separated. Imagination? Shadows in the rocks could adopt odd shapes to a worried mind. The old man must have meant something special to the youth or his need had been great.

"He wanted to talk," whispered Welos. "I knew it. I could see him but I couldn't hear him. I thought if I could get closer I'd make out what he was saying. He—" Pain contorted the features. "He—God, it hurts! It hurts!"

"Kill him," whispered Gartok. "Pass him out easy."

Rough mercy and the only thing to do. Dumarest reached out and rested his hand on the flaccid throat, his fingers finding the carotids, pressing them, cutting off the blood supply to the brain, bringing blessed unconsciousness and death.

Rising he said, "Let's get on with the war."

Chapter TEN

The song was one Lavinia had never heard before. It rose and fell with a wailing ululation which held all misery and pain and despair. A sound which grated on the nerves so that she screamed and clutched at her ears and then, as it faded, realized that it wasn't a song at all but the throbbing harmonics of the curfew which, sounding, promised for a while at least there would be peace.

Tiredly she rose from her bath. Always, lately, she seemed to need washing and always she was tired. A symbolic guilt, she wondered? A ritual cleansing? Or was it the subconscious desire to lave away the hurt and pain and to restore life as she remembered it?

A weakness—things were not and could never be the same. But some things would survive; the castle, the land, the dead who had never deserted her.

"A mistake, my dear." Charles smiled at her from where he stood against the wall. "You should have left things as they were. Well, no matter, soon you will be with me and then we shall have time to do all the things once you dreamed about."

Charles who had died long ago and who had been her early love. But now she had no need of him so why did he insist on returning?

"I don't love you," she said. "You know that."

"Do I?"

"Earl is my man now and for always. Leave me, Charles. You disturb me."

His smile thinned as his shape began to dissolve and became a part of the decoration of the bathroom. Delusia or had she almost fallen asleep in the warm water? Stayed asleep as she left the tub? Remained in a near-coma as she dried herself?

111

"My lady?" Her maid was at her side, her eyes betraying her concern. "Is anything wrong, my lady?"

"Yes. No. Bring me a drink. Something strong." Then, as the girl hesitated. "Hurry, damn you!"

The brandy helped, the stinging astringents helped still more, and the phial of pungent vapors which she inhaled finally drove the fuzziness from her brain. Did all women feel this way, she wondered, when their bodies became the receptacle of a new life? Her hands lifted to touch her breasts, fell to caress her stomach. And yet how could she be sure? There were tests which would answer the question one way or the other and yet she was reluctant to use them. It was an added joy to guess, to wonder if her missed periods were the result of love or physical disturbance, a baby growing in her womb or a metabolic upset caused by the fulfillment of desire. Such things happened to others so why not to her?

And who could be normal in time of war?

Bleakly she looked into the mirror as the girl dressed her hair, remembering, thinking of the wounded carried back into the castle, the dead cremated in heaps where they had fallen. Too many wounded and too many dead. Drugs and surgery could help the injured but how to replace the fallen?

War—a time of much sadness. Who had said that? Charles? No, he was the confirmed cynic. Roland? Perhaps when they had walked the upper promenade and he had touched her hand and mused on the workings of the universe. How long ago now? A year? A decade? A lifetime?

"My lady?" The girl had stepped back, her task accomplished, the mane of hair lifted and crested to show its bar of silver to best advantage. A crown for the smooth perfection of her face; shimmering, beautiful in its ebon profusion.

Would her daughter have such hair?

"It pleases you, my lady?" The girl was anxious, of late her mistress had been the victim of strange moods and sudden violences. "A touch more perfume, perhaps?"

"No." The girl had an animal-like instinct for preservation. The offer, rejected, had broken Lavinia's introspection by giving her the opportunity to make a decision.

Now she made another. "The ruby necklace and pendant earrings. The matching tiara and a ring. A large one."

Gens to adorn living flesh then, studying herself, she felt a sudden revulsion at her choice. Rubies—was she mad? At a time like this to wear the color of blood?

"Take these away." The jewels made hard, rattling noises as she threw them down. "Bring me pearls—no!" Pearls were tears of pain. What then? What? "The crystals," she finally decided. "Bring me the crystals."

Facetted stones backed by metallic films graven with lines to form a diffraction grating which reflected the light in glowing spectrums. An inexpensive novelty bought when she was little more than a child when bright and shining things had held a peculiar attraction.

As war seemed to hold a terrible fascination for men.

Madness, of course, a destructive urge which caused them to volunteer and to go out and face injury and death. Would women be so insane?

Her reflection told her the answer. Fight, she had demanded. Protect what is ours. Kill if it comes to that but stand against those who would rob us. Words—when translated into reality what did they mean? The answer lay in the infirmary whimpering in pain. Rose on columns of black smoke to the sky. Was in the red eyes of bereft women, the wondering gaze of deprived children.

When would it end? For the love of God, when would it end?

"My lady?" The girl was patiently waiting. "Is there anything else?"

"No." There was nothing else. Just a thing which had to be done because, once started, there was no choice. "You can go. No—a moment." Lavinia looked at the face reflected in the mirror, that of the girl's looking, it seemed, over her shoulder. "Do you have anyone in uniform?"

"No, my lady."

"No one? Not a young man?"

"Certainly not." The girl was offended. "That would be foolish, my lady. He could be killed."

"Yes," said Lavinia. "How right you are, girl."

Dressed, perfumed, adorned she made her way downstairs to find all her preparations wasted. Dumarest was not to be seen. Roland sat alone at the table crumbling bread into little balls with the fingers of one hand.

"Earl?" He shrugged at the question. "He's busy somewhere. Did you know they brought in a prisoner? They're questioning him, I think. Lavinia—?"

But she was gone and, again, he sat alone.

The room was small, bleak, lit with a somber light from suspended lanterns. A place with a bare, ugly floor, a table, a chair on which a man sat his body held by ropes.

He seemed little more than a boy then she saw his eyes, the way they roved over her body, and Lavinia knew this was no boy but a man slow to age with a cynical disregard for others and a selfish pandering to his own whims.

Dumarest glanced at her as she entered the chamber.

"Leave."

"Earl? Who is he?"

He said, again, "Leave."

"Please, my lady." Gartok was more discreet. "There is something which must be done and it may not be pleasant."

"Torture?" She looked at the man tied to the chair. "You intend to torture him?"

He was leaning back, smiling, his hair cropped and his nose uptilted a little. His clothing bore stains and the fabric over one thigh was red with blood. His lips were sensuous and his teeth even and white. Time would harden his features and rob him of the spurious youth—if he was given time.

"Earl?"

"I asked you to leave."

"And I asked a question." Then, as he made no answer, she added, bitterly, "Has it come to this, Earl? Are we to lose the very last scrap of decency? To torture a wounded man!"

"He has a choice. He could talk but refuses to do so."

"But he will talk," said Gartok. "He and I are in the same business and I know a man when I see one. He's made his protest and acted the part but now its over. Now he will talk. Right, my friend?"

"Go to hell!"

"You see, my lady, how stubborn he is? Looking at that

face you would never guess that he gouged the eyes from a helpless man and laughed while he did it. Nor that he shot an unarmed boy in both knees and left him to crawl over rocks as sharp as broken glass. I know him. I saw it done. And there was a woman—but I'd better not mention her. And he will talk, that I promise. Now let me get to work."

"Outside, Lavinia."

"You too, Earl." Gartok was blunt. "If I get nothing else out of this war I'm going to have this. Don't try to stop me. Just take your lady and go."

Lavinia was silent as Dumarest led her to the great hall. She remained silent as Roland rose, sat again as he was ignored to toy with more bread. A servant deftly served the first course. Irritably she pushed aside the plate.

"How can I be expected to eat?"

"And how can you expect men to be other than what they are?" Dumarest was harsh. "I told you once that when you hire men to kill you don't expect to get monks. Well, Kars is a killer and lives by his own code."

"He will kill that man?"

"Yes."

"And you allow it? Earl, what has come over you? Why are you so different?"

"Different to what? Did you ever know me when I too had to kill? Can I stop Kars? Do I want to? That man would be dead now if I hadn't saved him. I did it so he would talk. Well, he's going to talk and what he says might win us this war. Or would you prefer others to die in his place? Your maid, for example. Roland. Me."

"Not you, Earl!" Her cry was from the heart and Roland sensed it. Watching, Dumarest saw his hand close on the bread he was crumbling, tighten to mash it into a ball.

"Lavinia, calm yourself, my dear. Earl, what did you mean when you said there was a chance you could end the war?"

"It's a secret."

"From me?" Roland smiled. "Surely you trust me?"

"I trust no one. Lavinia, can we have some food?"

Protocol dictated that unless she ate no food was served. With an effort she mastered her distaste and the servants continued with the meal. Gartok appeared before it was

ended. His hands, Lavinia noticed, had been freshly
washed and his eyes held the satiation of a man who has
found an excess.

"Kars?" Dumarest relaxed as Gartok nodded. "So you
got it. Good. You'd better eat now. We'll leave in an
hour."

"Leave?" Roland shook his head. "You can't, Earl, and
you know it. The castle is sealed until dawn."

"Seals can be broken."

"But the Sungari—no!" Lavinia was firm. "No, Earl."

"We leave."

"But you can't." Her plate moved to fall from the table
as she pushed it with her arms; a gesture demonstrating
her agitation. "You know the Sungari are real. You know
how dangerous they are. We were caught outside at night,
remember?"

"And lived." Dumarest rose from the table. "And we'll
live again. Join me when you're ready, Kars. I'll be at the
raft."

Beneath the lights it looked something like an elongated
bubble, the opaque canopy fitted to the vehicle providing a
covered space in which to operate the controls. Discs of
transparency pierced it and apparatus had been fastened to
the outside; grabs and rams and pincers which could be
operated from within.

Dumarest had checked it by the time Gartok appeared.

"We'll lock in, open the doors and fly out," he said.
"Where do we hit?"

"There's a place on the Prabang estate. A collection of
huts used to train some men—you know it?"

"Yes." Dumarest glanced around the chamber. The inner doors were all sealed, aside from the two of them the
area was deserted, the outer doors which had been hastily
constructed were held by a single bolt which could be
thrown by remote control. "Let's go!"

The lights died as the doors slid open and the converted
raft edged into the courtyard. There would, Dumarest
knew, be a short period of grace and he had the raft up
and moving high above the ground before closing all but
one of the transparent ports.

"Why do that?" Gartok grunted his displeasure. "I wanted to look outside."

"It wouldn't be wise."

"Why not?"

"Just take my word for it." Madness waited in the night but how to explain? Trapped energies from the suns swirling in mind-disturbing vortexes? Some radiation emitted by the Sungari? Imagination and hallucination running wild?

"Like I did about the Sungari? They're as odd as the ghosts but, at least, the ghosts don't kill. Maybe the Sungari don't either? Nothing's happened yet."

"Give it time," said Dumarest. "Give it time."

He had lifted the raft high and sent it at top speed to their destination, sending it like an arrow hurtling through the night but, as fast as he was, the Sungari were faster. Something touched the canopy with a brittle rasping sound. It came again, then a shower of things which scraped at the thick plastic, rattling like hail, like thrown spears.

"What the hell is that?" Gartok reached for one of the ports. "Something is out there."

"The Sungari. Don't touch the port!"

"I want to see."

"Don't touch it!" The one Dumarest had used was now closed, the raft flying blind. "If you look out they can look in."

"The Sungari?"

Or the things they had sent. The last time they had been winged missiles constructed of chitin and tissue, barbed darts moving too fast to see, living machines programmed to attack anything in the shape of a man. This time they could be different but Dumarest doubted it. A good design was worth keeping and the creatures had proved their worth. But did they have abilities he didn't guess?

"Don't talk," he said as Gartok made to speak. "Don't move. Vibration could attract them."

"The engine—"

"Is a regular sound-pattern, unusual but different from a living organism. Words are something else. We can do without them."

Remaining silent as the raft hurtled on its way, the rasp-

ing of alien bodies gone now, the shape tested and passed
as a lifeless thing and not a deliberate breaking of the
Pact. A chance Dumarest had taken, a gamble he hoped
would succeed.

Before dawn, he thought. The journey should take them
long enough to arrive a couple of hours before dawn. A
good time, there was no need to wait longer than they had
to and enough would remain of the night. Reaching for
the controls he slowed the craft, mentally reviewing the
terrain below. There would be hills, gorges, flat places, ravines a range of mountains which they should pass to the
right.

Should pass, but if they had been diverted by the
shower of impacts or a vagrant gust of wind they could hit
and plunge to ruin.

Height would save them but the raft was small, the engine weak and the canopy had loaded the vehicle to capacity.

Cautiously he unsealed the port. Starlight shone like liquid silver on the ground below, shadows filling crevasses
and distorting perspective. Turning he stared to one side
and saw the loom of darkness against the blaze of stars.
The mountains were too close. The raft veered as he adjusted the controls and, immediately, it shuddered to the impact of a rain of glancing blows.

"They're back!" Gartok's whisper was louder than a
shout. "Earl, they're back!"

A gleam from the port, his face, a familiar silhouette—
how to tell? The movement of the raft even, inert matter
did not move in such a fashion. And yet still they could
not be sure. Animals roamed unmolested as the Sungari
gathered the night-mist but they were familiar. The raft
was not. But attacked it had not retaliated and was therefore harmless.

The human method of thinking but the Sungari were
alien and who could tell what motivations drove them?
They shared this world with men and that was all anyone
knew. A Pact had been made based on mutual noninter-
ference but who had made it and how it had been made
was forgotten.

Dumarest nodded, dozing, resting like an animal with

one part of him alert while the others rested. Then, checking the instruments, he knew they must be close.

"Kars?" He heard the man grunt. "Are you awake?"

"I'm awake." The man edged his way forward. "Have we arrived?"

"We're close. Better get into the armor now. You first."

Plates of metal which fitted close, articulated joints, helmets to protect face and skull. Normal protection for mercenaries engaged in close-quarter fighting and now it would be an added protection.

Again Dumarest opened the sealed port. The raft was still riding high and for a moment he was completely disoriented then he saw a crevass, a desert naked in the starlight, a formation he had seen before.

"We're going down," he said. "Brace yourself."

He dropped fast, slowing at the last moment, moving forward to halt, to turn, to dart ahead again as he found the huts. They were set in line backed by the cookhouse and stores all now tightly sealed. The raft landed between them.

"Now!"

Gartok was already at the handles of the external apparatus. A pincher moved out, closed, tightened.

"Up!"

A ripping as a section of the roof gave way. Down to fasten a grab, to rise again, to jerk one end out of the hut and expose the interior.

To move on and repeat the move lower down.

To slam the tough canopy of the raft against a wall.

To see emptiness and to taste the sourness of failure.

"They're gone!" Gartok swore as, in the starlight, he saw nothing but empty cots. "The damned huts are empty!"

"Could he have lied?"

"No." Gartok slammed his hand against the canopy. "No, Earl, no! He didn't lie. He told what he thought was the truth. He told me!"

Urged with pain, dazed, craving release—could he still have lied? Did it matter?

The raft jerked as something smashed against the port, glass splintering, showering inwards. The hole widened, plastic shredding, yielding to the things outside. Gartok yelled as a winged shape ripped past his visor, yelled again as it turned to slam with numbing force against his chest. Unarmored he would have died.

"Earl!"

"Out!" Dumarest dropped the raft with a jar. The vehicle was a marked target. "Head for the storeroom. Follow me!"

He staggered as he jumped through the opened door, falling to roll, rising under the savage impact of blows which filled his mouth with the taste of blood. The door of the storeroom flew open beneath the drive of his heel, light splintering from a lantern, the door slamming shut as Gartok followed Dumarest into the hut. It was heaped with empty crates and the air held the scent of oil and sickness.

On a cot a man reared upright snatching at a gun.

"Hold it!" Dumarest took a step forward. "Don't make me kill you!"

"You're human!" The man sagged with relief then broke into a fit of coughing, blood staining his lips and chin. He dabbed at it with a hand, looked at the smears, then dug beneath his pillow for a rag. "When you burst in here I thought—how come you made it through the night?"

"We were lucky."

"More than some. Three men tried it the first night here. Five more the following week and we lost two the day before yesterday. They went out and didn't come back." The man coughed again. "Just vanished. We didn't even find a bone."

"Where is everyone?"

"Gone." The man leaned back against the wall. His cheeks were sunken, his eyes bright with fever, the whites tinged with the blue stigmata of the disease which rotted his lungs. "They pulled out yesterday afternoon. I was too sick to go with them so they left me behind."

Dying, with a gun, to protect an empty store.

"Moved? Where?" Gartok snarled as the man made no reply. "Talk, damn you!"

"Or what?" The man shrugged. "You want to kill me then go ahead—you think I like being like this?" He coughed again and almost choked on the fretted tissue which rose from his chest. Dumarest found water, held it to the carmined lips, supported the man while he drank. "Thanks, mister," he whispered. "You going to kill me?"

"No."

"Just leave me here?"

"You've got food, water and a gun." Dumarest eased the man's head back to the pillow. "Which way did they go? North? East? South?" He watched the subtle shift of the eyes. "Any heavy equipment? Rocket launchers? Field-lasers? How about supplies? How many rafts? Did they get much warning?"

The man said nothing but his eyes spoke against his will, minute flickers, little tensions, signs which Dumarest had learned to read when facing players over countless gambling tables.

Gartok looked up from where he sat on a crate at the far end of the hut when, finally, Dumarest allowed the man to sink into an exhausted sleep.

"Well?"

"They moved out late in the afternoon, heading north and taking plenty of supplies. They had rocket launchers but no field-lasers. It was a sudden move—Tomir sent urgent word."

"Damn the luck!" Gartok glared his anger. "A day earlier and we'd have had them!" He sobered, thinking, "Rocket launchers, eh? Light or heavy?"

"Light."

"A strike force. Men able to live on what they carry, lightly armed, highly mobile, ready to hit and run. But where, Earl? Where?"

Chapter ELEVEN

In the infirmary a man was sobbing, "God help me. Please help me. Someone help me." On and on, a plea without end in a voice which sounded as if it had come from a broken machine.

A good analogy, thought Lavinia, but one she wished she didn't have to make. Too many human machines lay broken in the room now crowded with beds. Too many voices muttered and mumbled in droning susurations, sometimes crying out, sometimes falling into a low, animal-like moaning.

Why did they need to suffer?

She knew the answer to that; slow-time was expensive and in short supply. Other drugs were also in unusual demand. Injured men were doped and bandaged and left to heal in full awareness of their condition. Heroes faced with their folly—no, she was being unfair. They had fought for her and to mock them was to be cruel. They had the right to look to her for aid. The right to demand that she give it.

"My lady?" A woman, old, her face seamed and withered like the skin of a dried fruit, had caught her by the arm. "Are you ill?"

"No."

"You look pale. This place is not a good one for you to remain in. And it is bad for the——" She broke off, swallowing, realizing to whom she spoke. Women had a common function but not all of them enjoyed being reminded of it. "You must be careful, my lady," she ended. "Why not leave this to me and the others?"

The old and the young and those with the stomach to stand the cries and sights of pain. The injuries. The burns and sears and torn and ruptured tissue. The ruin of what had once been men.

And would be again, she told herself. Nothing must be spared, money, pride, nothing.

But what sacrifice could she make to equal theirs?

She forced herself to stand upright, to throw back her shoulders and smile, to move slowly along the line of beds, touching those who were awake, talking to those who could hear, resting her hands firmly on those who could not see.

And, even while she walked and talked and smiled she wondered. Had the old woman recognized her condition? Some, she knew, had the reputation of being able to spot pregnancy in its early stages before any signs were clearly visible. An intuition, a sixth-sense, something which they could read and understand. How else to account for the warning? The unfinished sentence which caution had broken short?

Were unborn babies affected by external stimuli? Would the atmosphere of the place affect her child?

Science told her that was impossible, but was science always right? Or did she want an excuse to stay away and her own hopes and imagination were hard at work to find one?

Outside the door she took a deep breath. Inside the air was clean and scented with pungent spices and sprayed essences of pine and roses but, even so, that outside seemed better, more wholesome, more pure. More imagination or had she a greater sensitivity than she had guessed?

Idle speculation and of no immediate importance but one matter required her immediate attention.

Roland looked dubious when she asked him to accompany her.

"Ride, Lavinia? Is it safe?"

"Safe? What has that to do with it? I must inspect the herd and select stock for breeding and for sale. It should have been done before." Would have been done if it hadn't been for Chelhar. "Well, are you coming with me or not?"

He insisted on caution, riding slowly, keeping armed retainers close, sending out scouts to check the terrain ahead. A caution which would once have irritated her but now she had lost the desire to gallop and it was good to amble along and enjoy the warmth of the suns and the touch of a cooling breeze.

Warned, the herdsmen were waiting. They had assembled the beasts and urged them past her in line so she could make her selections. Yenne, the master-herder, sat on his mount close to her side, brand-gun in hand ready to shoot colored dyes at her signal.

"That one!" she pointed. "That and that and that . . ." She glanced at him as he fired a blotch of ebon on the shoulder of a beast without her signal. "Why cull that one?"

"Weak in the legs, my lady. I've been keeping an eye on her. I'd hoped that her foal would be free of the weakness but it must be a dominant gene."

"The foal?"

His shrug gave the answer. Dead, of course, culled as soon as the fault was recognized. The mother, now caught in the general sweep, would shortly follow, bones, meat, hair and hide all put to good purpose.

The way of nature—only the fit and strong could be allowed to survive.

And the herd must be kept in prime condition.

As the animals passed and she continued to select the beasts Lavinia studied the old man. Later they would pick over the selection together for his final approval. It would be given discreetly, of course, sometimes by no more than the lift of an eyebrow, but he would not permit her to make expensive or stupid errors. But her attention had nothing to do with his skill or her determination to match it.

He was married, she knew, and had sired children. Would he have culled his own offspring?

Would Dumarest?

If the child she was now certain reposed in her womb proved defective in any way would he permit it to survive?

Small, yes, size was a variable. The color of hair and eyes was not important. The shade of skin would be determined by their ancestry. But if it were blind, or deaf or with a grotesque and swollen skull? If it had a split spline or misplaced features or internal organs wrongly placed? If it were a freak like some she had heard about which were displayed on barbaric worlds for the enjoyment of those with money to spend?

Dumarest would kill it.

He would do it with speed and love and mercy but the mite would die and so be spared the lifetime of agony and humiliation, the knowledge of inadequacy and the burden of handicap which had been its heritage.

He would spare it that, she was sure of it, as sure that she sat on her mount and watched beasts pass before her eyes. His face—she had seen it when he had killed. The face of a trait, not of a man, the naked determination to survive.

Would he condemn anyone to a life of hell?

She remembered the rumors of him having killed a wounded and dying man to give him peace. Would he deny that peace to his own child?

"Lavinia!" Roland was at her side, his hand touching her arm. "Here!"

She took the bottle he gave her and tilted it and felt the touch and burn of brandy in her mouth and down her throat. It helped ease the chill which had gripped her despite the warmth of the suns but did nothing to ease the turmoil of her mind.

A traveller, moving through the varied radiations of space, one who had spent years traversing the void and who had spent time beneath violent suns. A man who more than most had been exposed to the conditions favoring mutations.

What were the chances of his siring a normal child?

"Lavinia!" Roland's hand closed on her arm. "You shouldn't be out here. You're tired and worried. Dismount and rest for a while. Yenne can handle the selection."

"No." She took another swallow of brandy. "I'm all right."

"You looked distant."

"I was thinking."

Of Dumarest and his child and the moment which would come when she would show it to him and watch and wait—did all pregnant women feel this way? She would have to find out.

It was late when she returned and she was aching with weariness but when she saw the converted raft lying in the courtyard she went directly to the room which Dumarest

used as his office. He was alone, seated at a desk littered
with papers; maps, overlays, projections, lists. As he saw
her he rose and, taking her hands, sat her in a chair.

"You're a fool," he said, gently. "A good soldier
knowns when to rest. If you overdo things you'll fall sick
and we'll have another casualty."

"Don't humor me, Earl! Success?" She frowned as she
listened to his report. "They knew you were coming, they
must have!"

"It's obvious!"

"It could have been coincidence, that isn't important,
what is, is why they left?"

"To save themselves, of course!" She was annoyed at his
apparent inability to recognize the obvious. "A simple
matter of the need to survive you keep preaching at the
men. The wisdom of knowing when to hide and run so as
to fight another day. The doctrine of cowardice, I think it's
called, at least that's what my ancestors would have called
it. They believed in meeting their enemies face to face."

He said, sharply, "Who told you that?"

"About my ancestors? It's a matter of record."

"No, the other, the part about men being cowards if
they develop a regard for their lives. Who!"

"I don't know." She was startled by his sudden anger.
"Some talk, perhaps when I was in town, a rumor—you
know how these things happen. But does it matter?"

"It matters. It's a question of morale. Make a man feel
bad and you've half-won the battle. Make him feel foolish
and a coward to take care of himself and you've gained an
easy target. Was it Roland?" He watched her eyes.
"Suchong? Navalok? Taiyuah? A trader?"

"I don't know." She felt her own irritation begin to flower into rage. "Someone, somewhere, that's all I can say."

"Do you believe it?"

"That to be careful is to be a coward?" She remembered the infirmary. "No." Then, to change the subject.
"Where's Kars?"

"We went into town and I left him there."

"After news?"

"Yes. Now you'd better get into your bath."

"Later. I'm not a child, Earl." She looked at the clutter
of papers. "And this is my war too, you know."

"Are you enjoying it?"

"I hate it. I want it to end. That's why I wish you had succeeded last night. Earl, where did they go?"

A question he had been working to answer. From the heap he took a map, an aerial survey, the heights yellow, the depths green, ravines and crevasses made red slashes, deserts ochre smears. Stark against the shades of color were uncompromising black flecks.

"The stop-overs," said Lavinia as he touched them. "Are you sure?"

"Not certain but I'd put money on it." Dumarest used dividers to step out distances. "See?"

"See what?" She didn't apologize for her ignorance. "Tell me, Earl."

"It was late afternoon when they pulled out," he explained. "They headed north. That could have been a diversion but I don't think so. They didn't have time to waste. We can estimate the speed of the rafts. They were heavily loaded but there was a south wind which would have helped them along. Say they ran until an hour before dark. Not long enough to reach a castle but long enough to put them in this area."

She looked at the circle his finger made. "In the stop-overs. Of course."

They were thick-walled, barn-like constructions set at irregular intervals in the empty places. Buildings provided with food and water and emergency medicines for the use of those who may have been forced to land and had been trapped by the night. A relic of the old days when much travel had been by animal or foot. They could be sealed and lit with lamps burning oil. Their maintenance was the responsibility of the Family owning the land.

"They couldn't have all got into one," said Dumarest. "But they wouldn't have wanted to separate too far. That puts them here if my guess is right. It's the only place they could have reached where the stop-overs are close."

"On the edge of Taiyuah's land," she mused. "His grandfather tried breeding a herd there and built those huts for his men. Later, when he abandoned the idea, he turned them into stop-overs. That's it, then, Earl. We have them. Now you know where they are you can send a force against them."

He smiled at her enthusiasm but she had the naivete of a child when it came to war.

"I'm not certain they are there," he said, patiently. "As yet it's only a guess. But assume they are. If we attack on foot they would spot us and catch us in a cross-fire. If we rafted in they would blast us out of the sky with their launchers. And look at the terrain." His fingers illustrated his words, moving from shaded patches of yellow to red. "The place is ringed with hills. They'll have spotters on the summits and attack groups in the crevasses. Surprise is out and the rest would be slaughter. They're professionals. Experienced mercenaries. All we can send against them is barely trained retainers."

"They can kill, Earl."

"And have," he agreed. "But a lot of them got hurt doing it."

To be expected when men, flushed by the desire to be heroes, took too many chances. Wounded they would learn. Dead any lesson came too late.

"So what do we do? You can't just leave that force out there."

"Why not?" He shrugged at her expression. "Because they might attack or move? They can do that anyway. We can't stop them. All we can do is to keep them under what observation we can. If they're there we'll know it. If they make a move we'll know that too. But we can't do a thing without information."

And Tomir's had been good. Was there intent behind the move and, if so, what? An attack on Belamosk? Launchers could reduce the castle to rubble given time and assuming their crews would remain unmolested. But no commander could hope for that. A feint? Was he setting a trap? And the sudden pulling out, the luck Gartok had cursed. Luck or something else? A day earlier—but they hadn't known where to strike until the prisoner had been questioned. Tomir would have learned of his capture and guessed he would talk. Had the knowledge triggered the move? But why? Night attacks were unknown on this world. Who could have predicted one would be tried?

Cybers were masters of prediction—had one come to Zakym?

Ardoch stood in the open doorway of a chamber and watched a man play at the childish game of war. The room was old, the walls crusted with mineral deposits which seeping damp had piled on the stone, the floor uneven as the ground beneath had settled over the centuries. A place buried deep beneath Castle Prabang which now held the man who had made it his.

Tomir Embris who carried a false name and claimed a false identity. A clever fool—but one the cyber could handle.

"Ardoch?" Tomir lifted his head from the desk at which he sat. "I didn't hear you. Come and join me."

A board stood on the table, chessmen set in their squares, locked now in one of the surrogate battles which the man loved to play. He was large for his height, his body stocky, muscled like a bull. His head was almost a perfect round, the nose prominent, the eyes piercing. The greatest resemblance to his father was in his mouth and chin. From his mother he had inherited his thin mass of too-fine hair.

"Chess," he said as the scarlet robe of the cyber came near. "A game which should suit you. A matter of sheer prediction. Your color?"

Ardoch yielded the opening and, within six moves, knew how the game would end. Tomir lacked subtlety, seeking to crush and weaken rather than concentrating on the finer nuances of the play. A betrayal of a desire to destroy than merely to conquer yet never would he be able to admit to it as a weakness. A barbarian who would have been in his element leading a blood-crazed horde.

"You've beaten me!" He glared at the board. "In two moves—how do you do it?"

"A knack, my lord."

"As you warned me of the night attack? Was that another knack?" Tomir smiled and shook his head. "Of course not. You are trained to look ahead and to make the future plain. What was the prediction again? There would be an attack and the probability was in the order of eighty-one percent it would come when it did. And," he frowned, "what was the other?"

"The prediction that the attack would be made was ninety-one percent, my lord. The time was a greater variable."

"And the uncertainty was high." Tomir laughed with a harsh, barking sound. "I remember you saying that. High! But then you are never satisfied. Always you search for absolute certainty."

A mistake, no cyber would waste time reaching for the logically unattainable. Nothing was or could be wholly certain, always the unknown factor had to be taken into account remote as it might be. As the corroded wire in the generator of the ship which had carried him from Fralde and which, breaking, had caused delay. An incident which had led him to offer his services to the young conquerer who had snatched at the opportunity.

All that remained now was to capture Dumarest.

"Another game?" Tomir set up the pieces. "Let us look at this board as the field. Now, my troops are here and here. The enemy is there—a rabble hiding in a fortress. I can destroy it with missiles but will that win me the game?"

"The threat of destruction is effective only while it remains a threat, my lord."

"As is the threat of death. But what is the real objective? To conquer? To have the rulers of this world acknowledge me as supreme? Yes, I think so. Now how best to achieve that aim?" He paused as if expecting a reply. "You remain silent, aren't our interests the same?"

"My lord, in return for my help you promised me the man Dumarest."

"He's yours."

"Unharmed."

"How can I promise that? He insists on defying me. If he continues—what is the prediction that the Council will turn against me?"

"Ninety-six percent, my lord."

"So high?" Tomir frowned. "By my bribes and promises—surely they will continue to hold them back?"

For a fool the man had been clever but he had failed to look far enough ahead. Patiently the cyber explained.

"They were united in a common dislike of Dumarest as a stranger who threatened the status quo. That is why they were so eager to accept your claims. Dumarest was willing to sell and, had you been patient, there would have been no war."

"Why should I pay for what is mine?"

"You were not asked to pay but, had you been wise, you would have backed a loan."

"I didn't."

"And so the conflict. Dumarest knew you would attack but was confident he would receive support. He has been patient but that will not last. He will force the Council to give their support."

Tomir laughed. "How? What can he do?"

"He could, for example, dress his men in captured clothing and send them, armed and armored as mercenaries, to burn and pillage. You will get the blame."

"And they will give him—what? Raw retainers and a few inferior weapons." Tomir stared at the board and moved a piece. It landed with a small clicking sound. "Would he really do that?"

"Yes. The prediction—"

"Is high. I know. When? Soon?" Tomir moved another piece as the cyber nodded. "Even untrained men can be a nuisance," he murmured. "Guards must be maintained and the effective fighting strength diminished. And they could even hire an opposing force. Then we would really have a war."

Together with the waste and misapplication of resources which it would bring. A matter of small concern to the cyber but Dumarest would be involved and how to safeguard a man in the midst of a war?

"My lord, it would be unwise to permit the escalation of this conflict. The expense would be prohibitive and your reputation would suffer."

He was a commander who had failed to win a minor battle against servants armed with primitive weapons when armed with modern equipment and served by trained soldiers. The cyber was right; unless he won and soon his hoped for career as a leader was ended.

Thinking he set up the pieces on the board. How to win? How to force a surrender? There had to be a way and playing the game with its symbolic figures would help him to find it.

"It's your move, Cyber."

"No, my lord, yours."

And, unless he moved correctly, his life would be over.

Chapter TWELVE

"My lord, my lady!" The entrepreneur bowed. He was a small, smoothly rounded man with cool eyes and an ingratiating smile. A man of many interests who now dealt in the things of war. "Flame bombs of a new pattern which can be thrown or fired from a light-weight projector. Variable time-set fuses or impact detonation. The radius of effective destruction is thirty feet. The granules are adhesive and will burn through medium body-armor within five seconds. Secondary characteristics are metabolic breakdown of tissue together with the introduction of a nerve-poison. Truly a most effective weapon."

"No!" Lavinia shook her head. "To use such a thing against men!"

"A screaming mob can be a terrifying thing, my lady. And an opposing force, when faced with such devices, quickly lose their taste for combat. Am I not correct, my lord?" He waited a moment then, as Dumarest made no answer, delved again into the case his assistant had lifted on the table. "Miniature mines which can be dropped from a raft or sown from any moving transport. Each is the color of the terrain and will adjust by the action of photosensitive elements to acquire the exact shade on the place in which it lands. You see?"

He held out his hand and, as they watched, the egg-sized object he held took on the color of his palm.

"They can be adjusted for proximity detonation or impact; time-lapse or sonic sensitivity. They can remove the feet and legs up to the knees for an effective range of twenty feet. I can supply ten thousand of them packed in crates of two score dozen for a most reasonable price."

"Delivery?"

"Within a month, my lord." The man beamed at the

prospect of a sale. With luck he would be back in town well before dark. "Payment in advance, of course."

Dumarest looked at the case. "Have you anything else?"

A new model laser, a sleeve gun, some mortar shells, a gas, liquids which were light sensitive and would burst into flame when exposed to the suns. Kars Gartok grunted as the man lifted an eyepiece together with its attendant wires and pack.

"Don't waste time showing us that. No one has any use for light intensifiers on Zakym."

"No?" The man shrugged and Dumarest watched the flicker of his eyes.

"A moment." He held out his hand. "I'd like to see that."

"A recent innovation, my lord." The man was quick with his praise. "Not a light intensifier in the sense that it amplifies existing light-sources but something more. It scans the infrared areas of the spectrum and converts the pattern of received energies into a visible form. That alone would be an achievement though, as I will admit, not a novel one, but there is more." He paused to gain dramatic impact. "The scanners also resolve residual energy content on and within the object examined. To be short, my lord, with this device you can see in absolute darkness."

"Impossible!"

"Not so, my lady. What is light? A source of energy, yes? Therefore, as long as energy exists in one form or another it can be converted to light. Others have found the device most attractive."

"For night attacks, yes," grunted Gartok. "But we don't have those on Zakym."

"As you say." The man replaced the apparatus in the case.

Dumarest followed it with his eyes, remembering the flicker he had seen, the hidden amusement. Gartok had brought the man to Belamosk with him on his return from town and, from his expression, was beginning to regret it.

"I'm sorry, Earl," he said. "I thought the man would have something we could use. Everything he's shown us so far is too costly, too elaborate or based on a late delivery."

"Not so, my lord!" The man had heard. "I have other items resting in the warehouse."

"Drugs? Medicines?"

"Yes, together with antibiotics, hormone salves, re-growth mediums, skin renewers—all the things the wounded need to regain mental and physical health. An order for Khasanne where they are locked in a vicious struggle—"

"But which you are willing to sell if the price is right," interrupted Dumarest, dryly. "Immediate delivery?"

"Yes, my lord."

"Good!" Lavinia smiled her relief. "We have credit with the Nausi and there will be more when the herd is sold. If—" She broke off, recognizing the man's expression. "No?"

"My lady, I am a man of business. Expenses are high and profits small. To wait is to breed debt. If it were left to myself I would not hesitate but there are others, partners, you understand, who are not as confident in your victory as I am. And the load is spoken for and money is waiting. How can I explain my trust in your cause to those who are already using the money for a new enterprise?"

A lie, but the meaning was plain—no cash, no trade.

But she had jewels.

Dumarest led Gartok to one side as the man examined them. "Aside from him what else did you discover in town?"

"Little aside from rumor. Tomir expects more men and a few free-lances are looking for work. I gave them a half-promise. One of them told me that Tomir's equipment included long-range missiles for his launchers. And there was talk of a cyber."

"A cyber? When?"

"A while ago. He arrived after Tomir—something about a delayed vessel. I asked around but he seems to have vanished." Gartok shrugged. "Probably a mistake—a man saw someone wearing red and let his imagination run wild. I—" He broke off as sound filled the air, the rolling thunder of released energies which tore at the ears and filled the chamber with dancing motes of dust.

"Earl!" Lavinia turned toward Dumarest, her face startled, her eyes wide with shock and fear. "For God's sake! What's happening?"

Another explosion gave the answer, a third made it certain.

Castle Belamosk was under direct attack.

In his ear the voice from the combat radio said, "Nothing, Earl. I can't see a thing."

Roland, riding a raft following the foothills of the Iron Mountains, searching every inch of ground with high-powered binoculars.

Another voice, Gartok's, this time from close at hand, "Bare to the east. Not a man to be seen, not a trace." He sounded irritable. "I don't understand it. The bastards must be somewhere. And why the hell didn't they continue firing?"

A feint? But if Tomir had wanted to draw out the forces protecting Belamosk where would he attack next? And if he had wanted to reduce the castle then why cease firing before any real damage had been done?

Squatting in the raft Dumarest studied his maps, tracing the lines of suspected flight from the impact-points of the missiles. One had struck far beyond the western wall, another had landed close to the eastern side, more had dug craters in a wide-flung pattern to the south. The last had hit Ellman's Rest and blasted the old tree to splinters.

Each, he knew, could have been sent directly against the walls to blast a hole and bring down ancient stone.

"Earl?" Roland's voice again. "There's nothing here. Shall I return to the castle and supervise the work you ordered done?"

Cellars cleared, strengthened, stocked with food and water. The injured protected with bags filled with sand set along the infirmary and between their beds.

"Yes. Check with Jmombota about the drugs. Keep low—if you can see them then they can see you and a laser could burn you before you know it."

"There's no one here, Earl."

No one he could see, but Dumarest didn't bother to explain the difference, and the man was probably safe enough. Had units been placed on the attack he would have been shot at long before. Trigging the radio he said, "Kars?"

"Earl?"

"Rendevous as arranged."

The radios were part of the equipment captured from the mercenaries Tomir had hired and were probably being monitored. But Gartok knew what to do.

He stepped from the raft as it landed and strode to where Dumarest was waiting. The sunlight glinted from his helmet and body armor and gave him an appearance of ruthless, mechanical efficiency. Halting he scowled at the suns.

"Nearly ghost-time, Earl."

"We'll be on the way back before then." War, on Zakym, had to be carefully timed. "We'll hit one point, do what we can, then run. Prisoners if we can take them."

"Bodies if we can't. A stop-over?"

"This one." Dumarest dropped to his knees and unfolded the map. "I'm making a lot of assumptions and they could all be wrong but if I've guessed right we could catch them here. See?" His finger traced lines. "The trajectories could have a common origin here. The team could have moved between shots but I doubt it, they came too close and were too carefully aimed."

"They all missed!"

"That's what I mean. I think the misses were deliberate. Roland found nothing in the foothills and neither did you in the east. That narrows it to about here. They could have gone to there but they'll guess we'll figure that. So they could be just here." He tapped at one of the black flecks.

"Or rafted right out of the area."

"They didn't ride high or we'd have spotted them. Later when we searched we saw nothing. No, they are still close." Dumarest folded the map and rose. "Let's see if we can get them."

He took the lead, riding low, lifting the raft barely enough to skim the massive boulders and summits of hills. Behind him the half-dozen men forming his unit crouched low and remained silent. Those in Gartok's raft did the same. A small defense but it helped, sound and the glint of sunlight from equipment could attract instant attention where the soft, ground-hugging approach of the rafts need not.

A crevass drifted past below, a rounded jumble of boulders like the marbles tossed by a child tired of its play, a patch of gnarled vegetation. A turn into a narrow pass, a lift, a long, slow passage over the contours of rolling hills and then, at full speed, a downward glide to where a long, dark building showed against the ochre dirt.

"Out!" Dumarest hit the ground and rolled to the cover of a rock as his men obeyed. "Cover!"

He loped forward, dropped, signalled with a sweep of his arm, waited as shapes scuttled past to drop in turn while he searched the area ahead with narrowed eyes, rifle poised to fire.

Nothing.

The building was silent, the area around void of any trace of life. Gartok, landing to one side, lifted his helmetted head.

"Nothing, Earl. The place is deserted."

"Be careful!"

Men could be waiting, traps set, even now fingers closing on triggers ready to loose a storm of fire. Yet if present those men remained invisible and instinct gave no warning. There was no movement aside from that caused by a sudden flurry of wind; little plumes of dust rising from the acrid soil.

"I'm going in." Gartok rose to his feet. "Cover me."

Dumarest moved so as to increase his field of view. He saw the mercenary step cautiously towards the building, dodge around a corner, vanish. A moment later he reappeared, waving.

"A bust," he said as Dumarest came close. "The place is empty. You guessed wrong."

Not wrong—they had arrived too late. Kneeling Dumarest looked over the floor seeing the marks of booted feet and trails of dragged equipment. The doors had been open and wind would have carried dust to hide the marks had they not been recent. And a pot of coffee resting on a stove was still hot.

"Warned!" Gartok slammed his hand against the pot and sent it flying to fall in a pool of steaming liquid. "Someone ordered them out, but why? If they had known we were coming they would have had us in a trap. If not why the move?"

Khaya Taiyuah brought the answer, landing an hour af-

ter their return to the castle, arriving as the suns were low
and curfew was near. He was distraught, waving aside the
wine Lavinia offered to him as he was ushered into the
great hall. Waiting only for the servant to leave he said,
abruptly, "You must yield. You must end the war."

"What?"

"I bear an ultimatum. I had no choice, to have refused
was to have lost my worms." Bitterly he added, "For the
shame I ask your forgiveness. You are not a coward. But
the conflict must cease."

Dumarest said, "The terms?"

"Lavinia must yield and you must be handed over as a
prisoner. You will not be harmed—that is a promise. All
other prisoners will be exchanged. No compensation will
be demanded other than the cost of the forces involved. If
you refuse then Belamosk and other castles will be
destroyed. My worms—" He gulped. "The work of a lifetime will be destroyed. Everything will be lost. Everything."

He sat, a man suddenly older than his years, this time
not refusing the wine Lavinia set at his side. As he
reached for it Roland said, "The castle! What can we do?"

"Fight!" Gartok snarled his impatience. "So we lose
worms and collect bruises but that is war. An all-out offen-
sive starting at first-light. Every raft and man to sweep the
surrounding countryside and find those launchers."

An empty defiance. If Tomir had obtained the services
of a cyber the outcome of the situation would already
have been predicted and it was obvious what that would
be. Pressure exerted on Lavinia to yield. More to have
him handed over as a prisoner. The price of survival and
who would resist? Taiyuah afraid for his precious worms?
Navalok? Alcorus? Suchong? They would kill him to
preserve their castles. Roland?

"You can't resist," he said. "The very thought of it is
madness. They'll destroy the castle."

A bluff, but he didn't know that and could never be
convinced. Dumarest knew better. The Cyclan wanted him
alive for the secret he carried in his brain. The reason the
stop-over had been deserted, why no shots had been fired
at the rafts, why the missiles had fallen well clear of the
walls.

The promise would be honored. For how long was another matter.

"Earl?" Lavinia stared at him, her eyes wide. "What can we do? What do you want us to do?"

"It doesn't depend on Earl," said Roland quickly. "It's up to you to decide. If you agree to yield the war will be over. There will be peace. And what choice have you?"

"Earl?"

"We can fight." He glanced at the woman. "We could even win if you're willing to take the gamble."

"How?"

He said, flatly, "We ask the Sungari to help us."

Dawn broke with a scud of cloud which blurred the suns and threw a dull light over the upper promenade. Despite the thick cloak she wore Lavinia shivered, knowing the cold was less the result of temperature than trepidation. Roland, at her side, rested his hand on her arm.

"It's cold, my dear, you had best go below."

"No."

"What do you hope to see? Earl has gone with Gartok and we shall know nothing until the mercenary returns. And the whole thing is madness. Surely you know that? The Pact must not be broken."

"Is courage madness?"

"No, but a madman can have courage. Or," he corrected, "a blind determination which has that appearance. Why does Earl insist on continuing the war? He was willing to sell the land a short while ago."

"But not willing to be a prisoner. Why, Roland?" Turning she met his eyes. "Why should they want him handed over? And why should you?"

"I don't." He was quick in his defense. "I am only thinking of your welfare. Belamosk a ruin, the land ravaged, the herd slaughtered, and for what? Haven't enough men died as it is? If he loves you—"

"If?"

"—he will not want you to suffer. He will sacrifice himself for you as I would. And, after he has gone, things can be as they were." His hand tightened a little on her arm. "And I shall be with you, my dear. I shall never leave you."

"Neither will Earl."

"No?" He shrugged as if at the unthinking stubbornness of a child. "How can you be so certain of that? He is a traveller, restless, impatient to move on. What is he doing now? A thing of madness. To try and meet the Sungari and enlist their aid. To break the Pact and hope not to be destroyed. Fortunately the chances of him doing what he hopes to achieve are small. He could even die trying and, if he did, what has he gained? How can you trust that such a man will remain at your side? It would be best to forget him."

"That is impossible."

"So you may think, my dear, but you are wrong. Time is a great healer and the passing days erase even the strongest of memories. Soon after he has gone, it will be as if you had never met. Then, like a dream—"

She said, impatiently, "Roland, you are a fool. I am carrying his child."

"What?" He fought for breath. "No. You are mistaken."

"Time will prove me right." She missed the hurt in his eyes, the pain, too occupied with her own pleasure. "Be glad for me, my friend. You can see how impossible it is for me ever to forget him? Each day, each hour a part of him is with me."

"Does he know?"

"I hinted but I think he is convinced I was teasing. But soon he will have no doubt."

She smiled, thinking, imagining, the swell of her belly which would announce the coming life, the kick of barely formed, the stir of impatient life eager to be born. Boy or girl? A son or a daughter? No matter which, either would be an anchor to hold him fast. And there would be others to keep the first company.

"Lavinia, I am glad." She felt his hand resume its pressure on her arm and, looking at him, saw an emotion in his eyes she did not recognize. "As you say Earl will always be with us. His child if nothing else. Together we could watch it grow and teach it the old traditions of the Family."

"We, Roland?"

"If Earl does not return. If something should happen to

him." His eyes searched her face. "Are we to pretend it couldn't?"

As she had pretended during the long night when, alone, she had thought of him sitting, brooding over his maps, forming a plan.

A chance, less than one in a thousand, but a chance all the same. The only one he had if he hoped to escape the Cyclan and the trap he was in.

The caverns of the Sungari were unknown. They were a legend from the past. A scrap of history distorted, possibly, into fable. The things which killed in the night had never been investigated. The entire story could have been invented to protect the early settlers from the nocturnal threat.

And yet how often had he been told that Earth did not exist—and of all men he knew as well as any that it did.

And there were clues; a crevass containing a dead beast and a dead man, smoke which had stung his eyes and which had held a moving shape, a foal which had trotted from the smoke to vanish.

To vanish where?

He had been ill, dying, toxins flooding his body, the smoke catching his lungs and blurring his vision. A movement which had taken on the shape of a foal. But foals did not run alone and no mare had been close.

"There!" Roland pointed. "The raft, returning."

But without Dumarest. Lavinia watched as it landed and Gartok, jumping out, came towards them. Pearls of moisture glinted on his helmet and armor.

"Kars?"

"He found an opening, my lady. A cavern of some kind or a natural fissure. Earl wouldn't let me enter it with him. Said to come back and take command of the men." He glared at Roland. "I take it there's no argument?"

"From me? None."

Lavinia said, "Is there anything we can do to help?"

"We can pray, my lady. I'm not much good at it myself, but I'm willing to learn."

Chapter THIRTEEN

There were rasps and drips and small, rustling sounds, the somber beat of a drum and a liquid gurgle which could have been the pound of surf but which was, as Dumarest knew, the roar of blood in his ears.

As the drum was the beat of his heart, the rasps and rustles the scrape and movement of boots and clothing. The drips alone came from the outside world, the slow fall of moisture from the roof, its soft slide over time-worn stone.

A cavern which had opened from a tunnel which had led from a smaller cavern which he had reached by a winding fissure. Miles of endless turns and twists and descending floors. The weight of a world pressing in around him.

Darkness broken only by the ghostly shimmer of converted energies, residual forces amplified by the mechanism bought from the entrepreneur which he wore clamped to his eyes. In its field he saw the life-pattern of a lichen, something which moved and crouched against a wall, a shower of tiny motes which provided food for the lurking predator and which fed in turn on things too small for him to spot.

Water splashed as he pressed on his way. If the Sungari were here surely they would have noticed him by now. If the Sungari existed. If he were not plunging hopelessly into the empty world of caverns and tunnels which lay beneath the mountains.

And yet the flying creatures had come from somewhere.

There had to be a hive.

He stumbled and fell and climbed carefully to his feet. The apparatus on his eyes confused him a little but, if he should break it, he would be lost in total darkness to wander blindly through an unknown world. Halting he touched his waist, found the laser holstered there and drew it. Closing his eyes he fired at the ground directly ahead. Adjusting the gain from the light-amplifier he peered from between shielding fingers.

And looked at a palace of marvels.

Light streamed from the place which had received the bolt of energy, the stone still radiating in the visible spectrum, blazing like a sun in the infrared, emitting energy which was caught and retained by the walls and roof to register as a host of scintillating rainbows, each node a sparkling gem, each irregularity a vortex of luminous wonder.

A signal to the Sungari if they should exist.

Dumarest stood waiting, wondering if again the signal would fade to linger as a ghostly luminescence long after he had moved on. Another failure which would join the others he had placed along the path from the upper air.

And then, in his brain, something turned.

It was a numbing pressure which shifted as a worm would shift in loam, as butter would slide over butter, a wave move in the ocean, a hand turn in a hand. A thing which sent him to his knees, head bowed, sweat starting from face and neck to fall and sting his eyes to gather in droplets beneath his arms.

He heard the crying, the thin, pitiful wailing which seemed always to be with him.

And, abruptly, he was in space.

It was there, the stars, the fuzz of distant nebulae, the sheets and curtains of luminescence unhampered by the dulling effects of atmosphere. The void was all around him and he floated, alone in the empty universe as the air gushed from his lungs and the eyes bulged in their sockets and his internal organs began to burst under the pressure of boiling blood.

Dying as he had once died before.

As Chagney had died; died and still drifted, his empty eyes staring at blazing stars, his skin burned by the kiss of blasting radiations, dehydrated, frozen in stasis, still living, perhaps, somehow still aware. .

And crying . . . crying . . .

"No!" His voice was a gasp of pain. "No! No!"

Another voice, strange, remote, whispering in the recesses of his brain.

"A sensitive—quickly, the apparatus is erratic. Some malfunction and loss of integration . . . foreign elements . . . adjust . . . align . . . so!"

Coolness and the aching died. Peace came, the sickening movement within movement vanishing as did the blaze of stars, the fear, the crying, the pain.

Dumarest lifted his head and rose, trembling, aware of the aftermath of strain—aware too that his eyes were no longer covered by the amplifying apparatus.

Then how was it he could see?

The walls glowed with a soft nacreous light to either side. The floor was a dusty amber lined with green. The roof was bathed in an azure haze. The figure of the monk standing before him was a familiar brown.

A monk?

He stepped forward and stared into the cowl seeing a calm and placid face. Brother Jerome? Once he had known the High Monk, but Jerome was dead.

"And so no longer exists in the form you knew," said the figure. "But the shape is one you find comforting and trust. Why are you here?"

"I am looking for the Sungari."

"And have found them. We are the Sungari. You have broken the Pact."

With good reason, how else was he to ask for aid? And what good was a Pact when no one knew what it was all about? And how was it that an individual claimed plurality? And what was the real shape of the Sungari?

"You will never know," said the monk evenly. "And it is best that you do not. Yes, we have the ability to read brains. Those who first came to this world and contacted us used sensitives to communicate. We arranged a mutually agreeable settlement which you must know. Why did you not communicate earlier? We were watching you and your primitive attempts. Almost we destroyed you."

Curiosity had saved him—one thing at least men and the aliens had in common. And telepathy explained how they first had agreed to cooperate. The talent must have proved a recessive gene and had died from the surface culture.

Dumarest said, "How is it that I can see?"

"A direct stimulation of the brain. We also adjusted that which was in it. Life persisted due to the radiation of the twin suns. Now it is dormant and will eventually be absorbed but, while it lasts, we can communicate. You want something but what do you offer?"

Another familiar trait or was he misunderstanding the meaning behind the words? How to understand an alien mind? Yet some things all life had in common; the need to feed, to expand, to breed, to find safety. As the Sungari had found it by burrowing deep into the planet using the rock and soil as a barrier against the energy of the suns. Which meant?

"We are not native to this world as you have guessed. Long, long ago a ship was wrecked beyond repair. We did what had to be done and achieved a balance. When those of your race came there was attrition but finally we struck a new balance. Now you come asking for help and offer what?"

"Trade."

"How?"

"Items can be left for you to collect. In return you provide minerals and other sub-surface products. Later, if mutually agreeable, a closer cooperation can be achieved."

A hope, but what else had he to offer? As the figure remained silent Dumarest took another step closer. The robe the monk wore seemed to move and, stepping even closer, he saw that it was not solid material but a mass of tiny creatures shifting, each hooked to the other, their bodies providing the illusion.

As others made up the face, the lips, the eyes, the body of the monk.

A hive—but could things so small have the mental power he had experienced? Or was the figure merely an extension of a greater intelligence?

"Is the part the whole?" said the monk. "If you shear your hair is the hair you or are you the hair? If you should lose a limb which part is you? The part with the intelligence and brain? But what if the brain itself is in many parts?" And then, as Dumarest remained silent, "Do not try to understand. We are the Sungari."

Creatures from a different existence to that he had

known, perhaps bred on worlds men had yet to reach. Dumarest thought of an ant and its nest, a bee and its hive, a cell and the body to which it belonged. A brain commanding a host of appendages each able to convey information. A computer would be much the same and if its scanners were mobile and obedient—was the Sungari a giant organic computer?

More important—would it help?

"Come," said the monk. "You shall see."

And suddenly dissolved into a mass of glinting particles which rose and spread and spun a curtain before and around Dumarest so that he was enclosed in a sphere of shimmering brilliance which took shape and form and. . . .

He looked down at a world.

It was Zakym, the terrain was obvious but the conviction was stronger than that. He knew and, knowing, ceased to question. Hills moved to one side and a building grew large in his sight. Castle Belamosk, almost he could discern the figures on the upper promenade then, as he dropped lower, or appeared to drop, they grew clear.

Lavinia, Roland, Gartok huge in his helmet and armor. Others stood tense and watchful, some armed, others with empty hands. One was speaking but there were no words. Only vision as if he looked through the eyes of a flying scanner which, Dumarest realized, was probably what he was doing. Some creature of the Sungari flying high, seeing, relaying back what it saw. Something in a familiar shape or with transparent wings and body so as to be invisible against the sky.

Against the wall of the castle a flower bloomed with a gush of red and orange, wreaths of grey smoke rising to vanish, to reveal the ragged crater the missile had left. Others lay behind it; raw pockmarks in the dirt, each signalling the path of a creeping barrage. Soon they would reach the wall and send the massive stones to fall in splintered rain.

A blur and he looked at another castle, smaller, less graceful, less fortunate. A turret had fallen and one wall showed an ugly breech. The missiles which reached for it widened the gap in warning of what would come unless the ultimatum was met.

Already the owner must be on his way to Belamosk with what men he could find and arm. Navalok would join him, Suchong, the others. Tomir had increased his force by a simple threat.

Tomir?

He sat in a somber room looking at his maps, a communicator at his side and, behind him, like a scarlet flame, stood the cyber Dumarest and known must be at the commander's service.

And, this time, there was sound; the rustle of papers, the sigh of breathing, the rustle as Tomir moved, the scrape of his chair.

"Report!" he snapped into the communicator. "Unit Two!"

"No change, sir." The man had a hard, rugged face. "Still no surrender."

"Advance barrage."

"More and we'll be on the walls."

"Obey!" Tomir slapped at a button. "Unit Five! Report!"

"Castle walls breeched and internal damage achieved. Alcorus asked for permission to fly to Belamosk and urge surrender. Permission granted."

"Hold your fire. Unit Four?" Tomir grunted as he heard a similar report. "Maintain surveillance. Unit Three?"

"No reaction as yet, sir."

"Increase destruction. Cease only when the owner asks for permission to visit Belamosk."

Ardoch said, as the communicator died, "My lord it would be best to cancel your orders to Unit Two. Belamosk must not be put at risk."

"This is my war, Cyber!"

"And you will win it, my lord. But we have a bargain."

"Dumarest. I know. But he is stubborn and I refuse to wait longer. Once he sees his woman in danger he'll show himself. Once she sees her precious castle begin to fall apart she'll surrender. Either way we win."

A crude prediction, too crude for any satisfaction and

too dangerous for Ardoch's mission. One missile and luck
could send stone to crush Dumarest's skull. There was no
safety for anyone under fire. Even a near miss could ruin
his mission and, as he well knew, the Cyclan had no patience with those who failed.

He stepped closer to Tomir, unaware of the things lurking in the crevasses of the walls, the eyes and ears which
caught and relayed every word. Creatures of the Sungari
living in the gloom of the underground chamber, adapted
for a specific task and set to spy.

"My lord, you must cancel that order." His voice retained its even monotone but, even so, Tomir caught the
hidden threat.

"Leave me, Ardoch!"

"The order, my lord. You will cancel it." The cyber's
hand rose, a finger pointing at the young man's face. From
beneath the nail something gleamed and, as the hand
darted forward, pierced the skin of Tomir's cheek. "You
will do it now."

The man was already dead, the drug injected into his
flesh robbing him of all volition. He would obey as if a
marionette and then, like a puppet with broken strings, he
would fall.

But, as he turned to the communicator, his hand slipped
and hit the destruct button incorporated into the military
unit.

The unexpected. The unknown factor which could ruin
any prediction. The element which could render useless
any plan. Ardoch looked at his hand, the dead body, his
mind already assessing probabilities. The orders had been
given, even now the missiles would be closing the gap to
the walls. Orders could stop them but would they obey his
commands? Louchon was the the next in line, he could
stop the barrage, but first he had to be convinced.

Dumarest watched as the cyber left the chamber.

"Now! If you are going to help do it now!"

A wordless cry from the mind to those who had shown
him a little of the power they possessed. The Sungari who
alone could do what needed to be done.

And he was looking at a group of men standing around
a launcher.

They were efficient, glad the waiting was over, eager for

what spoils victory would bring. Their officer lifted an arm
and waited for a moment. He wore the visor of his helmet
raised and few of his men wore body armor. There was no
need when fighting at so far a distance. The sky was clear
of rafts, no enemy could touch them, and confident in
their safety they were careless.

"*Now!*"

Before the missile could be fired, the load it carried delivered to the castle, the fury of the warhead tearing at
stone and flesh and bone and turning graceful men and
women into crawling things of horror.

"*Now! For God's sake stop them if you can!*"

The air blurred.

It shook to the quiver of wings, the passage of bodies
spined and with serrated fins, creatures of chiton and
bone. Living darts, pointed, barbed, coming from nowhere
and striking without warning.

The officer screamed and fell, holes where his eyes had
been, blood gushing to stream down his face and join the
fountain pulsing at his throat.

His men spun, some running, others beating at the air
with hands too slow to hit the living missiles. They died,
falling with blood marking their bodies, clothing ripped,
flesh torn from bone, bone shattered by the bullet-like impact.

A shift and other men, more death, more destruction of
the invading force. And more. And more. Until, finally, it
was over.

From the raft the ground was a mottled patchwork of
rocks and boulders lined with crevasses and dotted with
patches of scrub. A hard place to find anything still less
the relatively small figure of a man. Sighing Gartok lowered his binoculars and palmed his aching eyes.

For two days now he had been searching without
success but stubbornly refused to give up. Dumarest was
alive, he was sure of it, and if he was alive, then somehow,
he would return to the surface.

The Sungari would help him.

"Sir?" The driver of the raft was young and proud at
having being chosen by the tough mercenary to handle the
vehicle. "Shall I continue in this direction?"

One way was as good as another but ahead reared the bulk of the Iron Mountains with the attendant dangers of turbulence and varying densities of air. Even an experienced driver could lose a raft in such conditions.

"No." Gartok made his decision. "Swing to the left and follow the foothills. Ride low and keep even."

Again he lifted the binoculars. They were fitted with an infrared detector and could reveal the presence of any living thing by its own body-heat, but the lenses remained clear.

"To the right," ordered Gartok. "Hold it!"

Something was over there and he tightened his hands at the hint of movement. A trace augmented by the sudden flicker of the detector. A living creature—Dumarest?

Gartok swore as a foal suddenly sprang from behind a rock to race down a crevass then, as the detector flickered again, yelled to the driver.

"Down! Down and to the right a little. Hurry, damn you! That's Earl!"

He was sitting on a boulder, his head resting in his hands, a thin coating of some kind of slime dried on his clothing so that he seemed to have been dusted with a frost-like powder. As Gartok approached he looked up.

"God!" The mercenary came to a halt. "Earl, your face!"

It was tense, drawn, the eyes sunken, the hair also coated with the lace-like patina. More rested on his cheeks, paling his lips, webbed on his eyebrows. It gave him the appearance of having aged a century; an illusion broken only when he spoke.

"Kars."

"Here!" Gartok had come prepared. He lifted a bottle and jerked out the cork. "Drink some of this." He restrained his impatience as Dumarest obeyed. "You found them, didn't you?"

"The Sungari? Yes."

"It had to be you. I told those weak bastards who came demanding that you should be handed over that. Told them and ordered them from Belamosk. By God, I'd have killed them had they lingered. Then I came looking for you." He added, simply, "I've been looking for a long time."

With others, scouring the skies with rafts, searching, always searching. But he, at least, had found.

"Earl?"

"It's over, isn't it? The war?"

"Over. Every last mercenary is dead. Tomir too, they found him in a cellar."

"I know."

"You know?" Gartok frowned, then changed the subject. "What are they like, Earl? Did they feed you? Give you water? How did you manage to persuade them?"

Questions followed by more and all stemming from a natural curiosity. Some impossible to answer while others could only be guessed at. The extent of the underground domain. The means by which access was gained to the surface. The method of breeding the selective strains which formed the extensions of the main intelligence—or had there only been one.

Was Zakym the home of a tremendous, alien brain?

One thing was certain, the Sungari owned this world despite what men may have thought. They, it, were the masters. Men were tolerated as a harmless insect would have been tolerated by a magnanimous gardener. But should that insect bite it would be crushed as men would be exterminated should they grow too fast and become too greedy.

Plague could do it. The destruction of all surface life, the crops and herds, would force them to withdraw. And there could be other ways based on the mind. Terrors which he could only imagine. Horrors without a name.

Dumarest rose and drank more of the brandy and felt the warmth of it spread from his stomach and restore some of his humanity. He had wandered too long in the dark, relied on the alien life-form too greatly, had suffered its probing too long. He needed to face those of his own kind, to hear voices, to take a long, hot bath and feel clean and wholesome again.

He needed to hold Lavinia in his arms and feel the soft comfort of her, the assurance of her need. But when they returned to Belamosk she was gone.

Chapter FOURTEEN

Roland came running to meet them as the raft landed in the courtyard. "Earl, how good to see you! And Kars! But where is Lavinia?" He looked from one to the other. "Haven't you seen her?"

"No."

"But, Earl, you sent word for her to come and join you!" Roland looked baffled. "I don't understand this. The messenger was explicit. He said that you'd been found and was hurt and wanted to see her. She insisted on leaving immediately. I wanted to accompany her but she refused to allow it. We'd had a small argument, nothing serious, but you know how determined she can be at times. I didn't want to upset her further so didn't press the point. But if you didn't send for her then who did?"

Dumarest said, "What did the man look like? Describe him."

"A big man, broad with a broken nose and scars around his eyes. He had a patch on the back of his left hand as if it had been burned at one time. I thought he might have been a herdsman."

"Flying a raft? Was he alone?"

"Yes. Of course, I should have noticed about the raft. It was stupid of me. One other thing, he had lost the little finger of his left hand."

"Louchon!" Gartok scowled as he rubbed the edge of his jaw. "He was with Tomir but I thought he was dead. The scars are the result of a cheap regraft and his hand once bore a tattoo. Someone didn't like the design and burned it away with acid. A year later that same man was found hanging head down over a fire. No one could prove who had cooked his brains but Louchon got the credit. A hard man, Earl."

152

One the Sungari had missed and he had served Tomir as had the cyber. If one was alive then so could be the other and it was obvious why the woman had been taken.

"Did the man say where I was supposed to be?"

"He mentioned a stop-over on the edge of Suchong's estate. The one near Eibrens Rise. I know it and could guide you." Roland was anxious. "Earl, what is wrong? Why should anyone have tricked Lavinia?"

"They wanted a hostage."

"But why? What value could she be? The war is over."

One war, but another continued and was just as fierce in its way. As yet he had been the victor but how much longer could his luck hold out?

As Dumarest turned to enter the castle Roland said, "Earl, aren't you going after her?"

"Later perhaps."

"Later? And you aren't sure? But man, she is carrying your child!"

"What?"

Roland gasped as Dumarest turned, catching him by the shoulder, the fingers digging deep.

"It's the truth, Earl, I swear it! That was why we quarrelled. I said you'd leave her and she was certain you wouldn't. Please! My shoulder!" He fell back, face drawn in pain, a hand rubbing his bruises. "You must go after her! You must!"

For a moment Dumarest stared at the man then, without a word, turned and entered the castle. Gartok caught Roland by the arm as he made to follow.

"Leave him."

"But he doesn't understand! Neither of you understand! Lavinia is being held at the stop-over. Tortured, perhaps, beaten, mistreated, put to shame. Doesn't he care?"

"He cares," said Gartok then added, impatiently, "Are you blind? Can't you see he's in no fit condition to look for the woman? He needs time to recover."

Time to swallow some wine and eat a plate of cold viands served by a smiling, bold-eyed girl. Time to strip and sink into a steaming bath, to lean back and try to relax, to ease the ache of muscle and bone. To remember the strange world of the Sungari.

To think over what Roland had said.

Lavinia with child? Her womb filled with his growing seed? Had it been a lie told to tease the man or the naked truth revealed in a moment of stress?

If so it was added bait for the trap he was certain had been set.

"My lord?" The girl returned with towels and vials of lotion. "Do you want me to attend you?"

"No." He softened the sharp refusal. "Did you see your mistress leave?"

"No, my lord. Are you sure I cannot attend you? A good strong rub with this will make you feel fresh and tingling all over."

"What is it?"

"A friction-mat, my lord." She held it up for his inspection. "We make them of woven strips of leather and special fibers from the south. Odd isn't it? It always reminds me of a handful of worms."

Worms!

Silkworms!

Yet Roland had mentioned Eibrens Rise.

Later, when dressed and rested, he sent for the man. Roland was adamant.

"I heard the name, Earl. I swear it. Eibrens Rise."

"I see." Dumarest looked past him to where Gartok was waiting. "Ready, Kars?"

"We can leave when you give the word."

"Then we leave now." Dumarest looked at Roland. "Will you come with us?"

"Of course. You need me to guide you to Eibrens Rise."

"No," said Dumarest. "To Taiyuah."

The place was full of creaks and smells, small sounds echoing in an oppressive atmosphere, the scent of vegetation mingling with the reek of something else which stirred and rustled and which lifted the fine hairs on the back of her neck with primitive distaste.

The worms, of course, she had never liked worms. Not since when, as a child, she had visited Khaya and had wandered off on a personal exploration and had got lost and found herself in a strange place fitted with tables and instruments and cages filled with moths and other things. Reaching for one she had knocked it over and showered her hair with wriggling creatures. Later someone had told her they had been silkworms but it made no difference. The name alone had been enough.

A long time ago and she had changed but Taiyuah seemed timeless. He had stood before her wringing his hands his voice carrying his shame.

"I'm sorry, Lavinia, but I had no choice. You must understand that."

She had been cynical.

"No choice, Khaya? Again?"

"My worms! They threaten my worms—how can you understand?"

A weakness which made him vulnerable. As her love for Dumarest made her vulnerable. As his love for her—but no, he was a different breed. He wouldn't come running to her even if still alive.

The doubt annoyed her. He lived! He had to live! To believe him dead was to help him into his grave.

And he had to be alive else she would have seen him in delusia. Nothing would have kept him away.

Stirring in her chair, dazed by the drugs she had been given, barely awake she murmured, "Earl, my darling. Earl, come to me, my love. Come to me."

And he would, Ardoch was as certain of it as he could be about anything.

Standing tall in his scarlet robe he looked at the woman, wondering at the madness of emotion, the insanity which defied all logic and flew in the face of all reason. A word and she had come running to fall into his hands. A prize which would gain another, more valuable, yet still reacting with the blindness of glandular impetuosity.

It was only a matter of time and he could wait. As the woman, recovering from the sedative, waited, saying nothing, listening to the drip of water, the rustle of things crawling on leaves. The cellar was chill and dank, a fit place to end the war she thought had been finished. Here would be fought the final battle. The hue of the cyber's robe was symbolic of blood.

Then she heard it, the slam of the door, a man's voice raised in alarm, the pad of booted foot. Quietly Ardoch moved close to her, his hand lifting to rest against her throat.

"Earl!" She cried out as he entered the chamber. "Earl!"

He saw her, turning, his hand dropping to the knife in his boot, freezing as he spotted the cyber, the position of his hand.

"Kars! Roland! Do nothing!"

Tension filled the room, giving birth to little sparkles which danced in the air, tiny motes of transient brilliance which glinted in a pattern of elaborate complexity. Flickers in the eyes registering the shift of electrons in the brain, the random motion of ions in the atmosphere. A hypersensitivity he had known before.

The Sungari? Here?

Dumarest looked at the walls, noting the cracks and fissures they held, each of which could contain alien eyes and ears. The chamber was below the surface and so within their domain. Did every room hold their spies?

Things which could adopt many forms.

Worms, for example—or men.

"Drop your weapons," said Ardoch. "Dumarest, you will permit yourself to be bound. Refuse and the woman will die."

Dumarest said, coldly, "What has that to do with me?"

"Earl!" Roland lunged forward to be caught and held by the mercenary. "Are you mad? Do as he says or Lavinia will die!"

"Then let her die." Dumarest didn't look at the struggling man. "I didn't come here to save her. She means nothing to me."

"Earl! For God's sake! She carries your child!"

"Keep him quiet, Kars." As the mercenary clamped his hand over Roland's mouth Dumarest said to Ardoch, "Is Louchon waiting at Eibrens Rise with men and gas to stun all who arrive? Did you think me fool enough to swallow such a story?"

"The prediction was high in order of probability. But if you are not interested in the woman why are you here?"

"For you," said Dumarest. "For money. Charl Embris will pay a high reward to the man who delivers to him the murderer of his son."

A bluff? Ardoch stood, assessing the situation. How could he have been so greatly at fault? Every factor had been calculated and an extrapolation drawn from viable premises. Yet, as he had so often reminded his clients, always there was the unknown. And had he been so much in error? Dumarest had come as predicted—only the motivations driving him seemed to be at variance. Greed instead of love. But had the act been witnessed or was it nothing but a wild guess?

Dumarest, watching, saw the almost imperceptible movement of the hand resting against Lavinia's throat.

Dryly he said, "I trust you remembered to reload the needle buried beneath the nail."

Proof if any was needed. Weight to add to the logic of Dumarest's actions, his apparent unconcern for the woman. Why should any man sacrifice himself for another? Why should any rational being be so insane?

And why did the room keep flickering?

Ardoch blinked, aware of a peculiar tension in the base of his skull, a stirring as if the grafted Homochon elements were rising from quiescence. Colors glowed with a new brightness, hues merging, shifting, altering the tone of skin and hair, touching the chamber with alien configurations.

But he was unprepared . . . the Samatchazi formulae . . . the relaxation . . . the defenses against invasion . . .

His mind expanded, bursting with an overwhelming flood of sharpened impressions, opening like a flower to the rays of alien suns.

Burning . . . burning . . . dying in a flash of unbearable revelation . . . a sac overfilled . . . the filament of an overloaded bulb . . . searing . . . torn with mental corrosion. . . .

Ardoch reared, rising to stand on the tips of his toes, head thrown back, mouth open, arms extended, the sinews of his neck standing like ropes against the skin. His eyes were glazed, blind, and the pupils uprolled so that only the glisten of white showed between the lashes. From his open mouth came an animal-like panting. A mewing. A wordless, mindless drone.

And, standing, he burned.

Smoke rose from the skull-like head, streamed in oily tendrils from the sleeves of the scarlet robe, hung in a noxious cloud so that his figure became blurred and sagged as if made of wax, flesh falling from bone, the bone charring, turning black, becoming ash.

Falling.

Falling to lie in a small heap on the moldering floor.

To rest in a silence broken only by Lavinia's hysterical screams.

Three ships waited on the field and Dumarest had already made his choice; a compact vessel which would take him beyond the Rift and on to Izhma. A world where he would find computers and a society free of traditions, a planet on which the dead stayed that way and delusia was unknown.

Gartok said, "Well, Earl, I guess this is goodbye. But who knows? Someday we may meet again."

"When you get tired of the fleshpots, Kars?"

"Things are easy here," admitted the mercenary. "And a strong man can make his way if he is willing to abide by the rules. But, one day, it'll get that I want to see the stars. That'll be the time for me to leave."

As it was time for Dumarest to leave but he had more reason than a need to see the stars. A cyber had died and the Cyclan would know it. As they must know he was on Zakym. Others would be sent to find the trail and, again, the dogs would be on the chase.

"They'll learn nothing from me," said Gartok, quietly. "Nor from anyone else on this world. How many really knew you? How can they tell more than is already known?"

And how much did he know?

Dumarest looked at the man, seeing the scarred face, the flat, impassive features, but seeing more than lay on the surface. Like Zakym the man held an inner life; one that was shrewd and more complex than the one he displayed. An arrangement with the Church, he had said. Monks did not advocate violence and abhorred killing but justice was dear to them. Even poetic justice.

"The Sungari," said Gartok, abruptly, as if wanting to end the scrutiny. "They took care of the cyber, yes?"

Driving him insane with the stimulation of his brain, showing him vistas beyond imagining, using him, probing, discovering. Investigating the unusual specimen.

Testing him to destruction.

"Burning him." Gartok shook his head. "I'll never forget that. "Turning a living man into ash while we watched. Maybe he deserved it, but, God, what an end! But why, Earl? Why?"

"They are curious," said Dumarest. "I appealed to that curiosity. And they could have wanted to show just how powerful they are. Remember that, Kars, if ever you are tempted to cheat them."

"I will."

"I think they wanted to complete the bargain they had made with me. We found Louchon dead later—he and the cyber were all that was left of the invading force." Dumarest added, casually, "You're staying at the castle?"

"Where you should have been, Earl. Lavinia—"

"No." He hadn't seen her since the time the cyber had burned.

"She could be made to understand. You had to reject her. I knew that and even Roland came to see it was all you could have done."

"But he hasn't said so?"

"No." Gartok rubbed the edge of his jaw. "I didn't trust that man. I thought he was working with Tomir—but it was Taiyuah who did that. Him and his damned worms! Well, he's old and will be dead soon."

Dead and forgotten and his petty intrigues ended. But others would live, Roland for one.

"He loves the woman," said Gartok. "You were right, Earl, the man is sick with longing for her. And I think that now she knows it. He was the only one who showed concern. And yet—how can anyone change so soon?"

They didn't. She hadn't. But time would work its magic. She would forget or, if not forgetting, cease to consciously remember. New life would come to fill her days and Roland would be there to provide the father and comforter she and the child would need.

His child.

Born on this strange and alien world. To grow in comfort and security as all children should. To be happy as was their right. The son or daughter he would never see.

A siren wailed from the field and Dumarest held out his hands. Gartok touched them with his own, palm to palm, the mercenary salute of friendship showing the lack of weapons.

"Good luck, Earl."

"Goodbye."

Gartok watched as Dumarest headed toward the gate, passed through it, moved across the field to the waiting ship. A man escaping from a world which had become a trap—but one still locked in the prison of his dream.